CHASING
THE BEAST

CHASING
THE BEAST

RUSSELL BROWN

www.blkdogpublishing.com

Other titles by Russell Brown

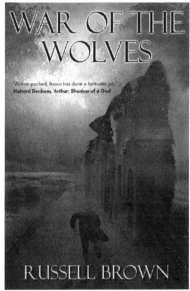

War of the Wolves

For Fiona, my editor-in-chief.

I couldn't have done it without you.

Prologue - the end

I looked down the barrel of the pistol and licked my lips. My arm shook from the top of my shoulder to the tips of my icy fingers, each one latched tightly around the grip of the sleek weapon. The wind caressed them gently, shivering over scratches and cuts, tickling my blackened nails, caressing my thumb, and urging my trigger finger to press down. Intermittent gusts pushed at the small of my back, rocking me forward, shaking my stance and grabbing at my gun arm.

'Why are you doing this?' I said. 'You're not going to get what you want. You must know that? People have died. The police are on their way and you've got nothing to show for all the pain and suffering you've caused. You might as well turn and run; it's your only chance.'

'The pain and suffering is what I wanted, don't you understand?'

'I understand that you're a monster, causing nothing but harm. But this all stops now. I've got the gun, remember.'

'You're not going to kill me. You don't have it in you. I've seen how you operate. You wouldn't hurt a fly, you don't have the strength. It takes a special kind of courage to shoot someone and all I see stood in front of me is a coward. A coward who would chase someone across the countryside rather than face up to what they have to do. I'm worth ten of you and you know it. I wouldn't have even asked. You'd be dead right now if I was standing in your place.'

I pulled the hammer back and prepared to squeeze the trigger. The wind gusted again, racing through the tall grass surrounding us. It whipped around my trouser legs and wrapped my shirt tightly around me. It urged me forward. It urged me to pull the trigger. It demanded that the chase come to an end.

'You think it takes courage to shoot someone?' I said. 'It doesn't take courage; it takes rage!'

I squeezed the trigger and a moment of fire exploded from the cylinder. The gun recoiled in my hand, jumping upwards, sending my gun arm reaching for the sky. The blast ricocheted outwards, echoing around the sand dunes and fanning through the grass.

1 - THE CHASE

I lay in the hollow, looking up at the clear blue sky and realized I couldn't remember how I'd gotten there. I remembered getting up and having breakfast. I remembered the taxi ride into town and the smells from the market stall, each one accompanied by the cheerful shouting of a vendor. I even remembered the first feelings of panic and that small voice in the back of my head telling me that something was wrong. After that, all my memories seemed to roll up into one continuous kaleidoscope of pain and suffering. Now here I was, lying in a hollow, looking up at the clear blue sky.

I was lying as flat as I could, in an attempt to show as little of my body as possible to the outside world. Before flinging myself to the ground, I'd noticed that the field rose gently to the brow of the hill, the top crowned with a small copse of trees. I could hear the wind gently playing through the ears of corn that bordered my hiding place and, in the distance, the sound of cars whispering as they passed. The sounds gave my mind a small period of peace, a space in which to think. My breathing was finally even and steady for what seemed like the first time in an age; no more ragged breaths ripping through my chest as I fought to keep up. No more sobbing gasps as I tried desperately to keep my eyes fixed on the blue coat in front of me.

I did a quick inventory while I lay there. My watch was broken, my mobile dead. My clothes were smeared with dirt and sweat stains. My hiking boots, new on just yesterday, were scuffed and smeared and killing my feet. I could feel tight, congealed blood resting above my left eyebrow. My hands were crisscrossed with thin ragged red lines and a memory of a thorn bush suddenly flashed before me. My nails were caked in dirt and my calves ached from all the chasing. All things considered I didn't think I was in too bad a shape.

I lay my head back down on the hard-packed earth, enjoying the blissful experience of finally being able to rest my tired body. I knew I would have to move soon, but I didn't want to leave my shelter just yet. I briefly considered reaching for my backpack to see if there was any water inside but rejected the idea. It would mean I would have to show too much of myself above the hollow's rim.

Sighing quietly, I tilted my head upwards once again to watch as the trees swayed gently in front of my vision. The lazy branches playing across the azure blue sky, the deep green leaves standing in stark contrast to the brilliant blue. While I lay watching this peaceful scene, the branch reaching out furthest across my sanctuary suddenly exploded in a spray of wood and leaves. Debris fell all around me, covering my face for the briefest of moments. I reached up to brush away the rubble and wrenched my arm downwards as I felt something brush past the sleeve of my coat. Two more mini explosions punctured the ground on either side of me, spraying clouds of dust and dirt into the air.

The force of my fear flattened me against the earth, my heart racing once again, electric currents running through my body, stinging my skin to life and lifting the hairs on my arms. I screwed my eyes shut and prayed that the hollow would give me enough protection, hoping that it wouldn't turn out to be my grave. I could hear the sound of my heart thumping against my rib cage, playing a melody of fear in concert with my quick breathing. Nothing happened for several heartbeats and I opened my eyes and let the light flood in. I couldn't be sure why the shots had suddenly rung out. I didn't know if they were a serious attempt at killing me or a warning to stay where I was. Either way, I knew I had to move soon. Any delay would give him an opportunity to escape and I couldn't allow that. I took a deep breath to steady my nerves and prepared myself for what I was about to do.

'What are you thinking, Dan? It's a very dangerous thing to do,' my dad whispered between my ears.

'I'm running after someone with a gun. Someone who's trying to kill me, that's what I'm doing,' I replied to the air.

Not a very sane thing to do, but my only option. I couldn't let him get away, not after what he'd done.

I took another quick look at my watch before realizing, once again, that it was broken. I hated not knowing how long this had been going on, how long I'd been chasing him and how long I'd been like this, waiting for him to move on or shoot me. I was sure it could only be a matter of minutes but it seemed like hours.

I took a deep breath and flung my body in a 180 degree whirl, so I could rest on my stomach. I was now in a better position to raise my head above the rim of my hiding place. Drawing in another breath, I raised myself up quickly and scanned the horizon. All was peaceful, a country scene at the height of summer's bloom. The corn swayed gently while the trees at the top of the hill stretched their branches up to the sky in mock surrender. Nothing gave an impression of the hurricane that had just passed around me.

I pursed my lips and tried to decide what to do next. Another quick look decided it for me. I saw a flash of blue retreating as he made his escape.

I jumped up from my hiding place with a start, panic tightening my stomach and sending bile into my mouth. He was getting away, that was all I could think about. I didn't consider the fact that this might be a bluff and he could turn at any moment and attack me. For all I knew, he was already racing across the next field, racing away, racing towards freedom.

I had the presence of mind to crouch down and scoop up my back pack, slinging it around my shoulder without a second thought. My legs were already leading me away, starting my route up the side of the field. I kept close to the hedge as I ran, trying to use its cover as some sort of protection. The tangled thorns tugged at my clothes as I pushed forward, my feet crashing through the green petals of a thousand sweet violets As I reached the top, I lowered into a crouch then flung myself down against the pitted side of a mound of earth. Hoping that the rutted sides, turned over by years of ploughing, would give me some sort of protection. I was breathing heavily after my efforts but felt strangely elated to be away from my hiding place. Even with a gun he hadn't been brave enough to turn and face me.

I lay there waiting, until the pounding between my ears subsided. I may be in mortal danger lying there like some fatted pig wallowing in the mud but I had to take the chance; he couldn't get away. Taking in another huge gulp of air I rose and launched myself forward. This was my first mistake and one that saved my life. The tip of one of my walking boots snagged on the lip of the mound of earth that, only moments before, had given me protection. I stumbled forward, falling heavily onto my stomach, legs flailing behind me as I fell. I was instantly aware of a whizzing noise as a bullet passed through the space I'd just vacated.

Panic grabbed hold of me, wrapping its icy fingers around my heart. I was out in the open. He could take careful aim and finish me off. Instinctively, I rolled sideways and away from where I thought he might be hiding. Clumps of earth and dried grass exploded into the air as more bullets ripped into the ground. I rolled my body again in a desperate attempt to avoid them, throwing myself up against the trunk of a nearby tree. I curled my legs into my chest and waited for the inevitable bullet to rip into my body.

Nothing happened.

The wind rose in a quiet whisper, rustling amongst the grass and weeds and tickling the leaves on the trees. He could have run out of bullets, or more likely was taking his time reloading his gun. I knew he had more than the half dozen held in the chamber. He had to have been considering how many he'd shot at me. I had to take the chance to move to better cover as soon as I could, and certainly before he had time to reload his gun. Taking a quick look around, I noticed an ancient pile of stones nestling against a screen of bushes off to my right.

I uncurled slowly, getting ready to rise and launch myself over to them. I knew this would be the most dangerous part; I'd be out in the open, a nice big target. It couldn't be any easier for him if I'd put a target on my back. Without thinking, I rose to my knees and propelled myself forward.

That was my second mistake. Bullets hit the ground around my feet and I tripped once again, hitting the side of the stones with a bone-jarring crunch. Without thinking I managed to put the stones between myself and Bluecoat, then lay there feeling vulnerable and alone. For a time all I could hear was the sound of my breathing coming in and out of my lungs. I tried to listen out for any other sounds, particularly any danger coming towards me, but my internal sirens were too loud.

Eventually I leaned out from the side of my hiding place, to see what was happening, half expecting to see him striding towards me, gun in hand. But the view was empty save for swaying trees and whispering grass. I leaned back and sighed in frustration, where had he gone now?

2 - LOOKING DOWN THE RABBIT HOLE

'I like bullets.'

'Yes I know you do, especially the ones you shoot.'

'Of course, they're the best, they're the ones sent with love.'

Two shadows draped down into the bottom of the hollow, their outlines writhing like a nest of vipers as the grass was brushed by the wind.

'It looks like he was here for a while. The grass at the bottom is quite flat and there's a lot of bullet holes,' said the first shadow.

'Do you think it was a fierce battle?' asked the second shadow.

'Not unless they were both armed and I suspect that was not the case.'

'It's amazing our new friend isn't dead already, then,' said the second shadow.

'Amazing indeed,' replied the first.

'Where do you think they've gone?'

'Up and over, it would appear. Both seem to be very determined; well, you would be in such difficult circumstances, wouldn't you?'

'Yes, you would indeed.'

'Up and over it is. Let's take our time though. No need to intrude on their private pain just yet, what do you say?' asked the first shadow.

'Oh yes, no need to intrude just yet,' replied the second.

3 - A KILLING FIELD

I leaned against the stones and tilted my head towards the sky. Letting the sun warm my face and ease my aching shoulder. Suddenly I was hit with an awful thought. I was letting him get away. Rising quickly, I picked up my backpack and made my way around the pile of stones. I wasn't worried about getting shot, I was sure he'd already gone. I waded through tall grass and made my way into the quiet shade of the woods, hardly seeing the green and brown splendour surrounding me, my thoughts already whirling with questions. How was I going to catch him, what would I do when I did? Was it revenge I was after or justice? I'd convinced myself it was the latter as I'd raced after Bluecoat throughout the day. Now I wasn't so sure. Pleasant thoughts of his pain and suffering began to linger in my mind. When I caught him I would make him pay. That's what I promised myself. That's what I'd promised my dad. The thought of him sent another spasm of pain and longing racing through my body.

Breathing deeply, I made my way slowly through the trees, skirting a family of daisies as I went. Reaching the edge of the tree line I took a careful position behind the bole of a sturdy ash and looked out at a farmer's field running gently away from me. Nestled at the bottom was a farm house and out buildings. A scattering of lazy cows meandered in a field next door and an abandoned red tractor nestled in a clump of weeds. It looked idyllic, but if this had been the way he'd gone then I knew it for what it really was – deadly. Any one of a million places could be holding a sniper and his gun and there was a nice wide open space between me and the edge of the farm. This had to be crossed first. On any other day it was just a patch of earth; today it was a killing field.

An old trail, rutted and worn, wound its way gently down the slope, disappearing behind a rusted red gate at the bottom of the hill. I couldn't be sure if this was the way he'd gone and was risking a lot on a guess. I shook my head and gazed down at the ground. That's when I noticed it, a small glint of gold shining in the sun. The bullet looked out of place next to the deep green of the grass it sat in. I picked it up and rolled it between my finger and thumb. Its smooth surface was tarnished by oily prints, mine and his. I could almost feel his shaking fingers gently griping the cartridge as he tried to send it into the barrel, gasping behind his hiding place and praying that I would eventually give up. This was all I needed. I had no more doubts. He had come this way and he was hiding somewhere in the farm. I knew what I had to do. I had to get to the bottom of the field and through the red gate without getting killed; simple!

'You have to be careful, Dan, this is a terrible chance you're taking,' my dad warned.

'I know, but it's that or the funny farm, Dad, which would you prefer?'

He didn't respond.

The only way down was straight and dangerous. But I had a plan, simple and quickly thought out and it depended on my reaching the bottom of the field unhurt.

'One last chance, Dan; are you sure there's no other way?'

'I'm sure, there's no other way, now, shut up!'

Setting my head straight and my shoulders down, I took my first step into the field. There was only one way to get down to the farm and that was to walk – straight and in full view, it was reach the gate or die in a hail of bullets. Small dust clouds curled around my boots as I walked onto the brick hard field. The heat rose suddenly and I realised I was out of the shadows and in full view of anyone looking up from the farm. My heart began to rattle in my chest and my mouth suddenly seemed as dry as a desert. My clothes were hot and cloying, tightening around my body like a shroud. My body started to shake despite the heat, a quick and fast vibration rattling me to my bones.

I could hear every sound in perfect clarity from birds and insects to the sighing breeze. Colours stood out in brilliant contrast, violent greens and blues set against the deep brown of the earth stretched out before me. I felt dizzy and light headed as I made my way forward. 'That's just the lack of food and rest,' I murmured to myself. My arms and legs seemed too big for my body. I wasn't walking down the field, I was stumbling down it, one heavy foot at a time. It took every effort I had to move forward, to move towards the gate. Electric currents once again charged through my veins, my bladder was full, my body ached and I wanted desperately to be anywhere else.

I expected to hear the crack of a gun at any moment and wondered if I'd hear the sound before the bullet hit me in the chest. Where would it hit, my chest, my head, my stomach? Maybe he'd miss or the wind would take the bullet past me. Perhaps he'd aim for my legs, trying to slow me down or warn me to stop and turn around? My mind was a whirl of possibilities as I gradually and deliberately made my way down the field. At some point, while my mind was racing and I was sweating and stumbling, I realized I was half way, then I started to run.

The possibility of surviving this suicidal chase made me more afraid than ever. I could almost cope with the idea that I wasn't going to make it. Part of my brain had already accepted that it was all going to end here, out in the open, under the burning sun. But to be so close to surviving made me more afraid than the thought of getting shot. I was panicking now, running at full speed down the hill, my arms and legs cart wheeling around as I raced over the uneven ground. My breathing drew in and out in uneven, ragged gasps, my chest heaved and my head wobbled uncontrollably from side to side.

As I reached the bottom, I veered away from the gate,

heading towards the building that was nestled against it on one side, hoping against hope that he hadn't waited until now to take aim and shoot me down. I raced across the front of the gate, the sound of my boots digging into the earth seemed as loud as cannon fire. Surely he could hear this, surely now he was going to shoot?

I ran alongside the edge of a small, squat building that looked like an old barn of some kind, made out of brown stone, crumbling and weathered with age. I skidded to a halt and turned to face the gate, now only visible as a red slash running parallel to the barn wall. Resting my hands on my knees I doubled over, gasping for breath, my head pounding, the sound of the surf raging in my ears. In between gasps, I looked around and saw the field stretching up and away from me. Only then did I realise just how far it was and how exposed I'd been. He could have brought me down with ease almost any time he wanted, but he hadn't.

'What the hell?' I gasped, my stomach aching with the strain of filling my lungs with air. 'Where the hell is he?' I asked the blue sky, but for the first time that day, my mind didn't reply.

4 - Up and Over

I raged inside with frustration, the only sound my ragged breathing, clawing in and out and filling my lungs with much needed air. I'd made it all the way to the bottom, risking life and limb in the process and he hadn't tried to shoot at me once. A single question tumbled over and over inside my brain; where was he? I contemplated rushing forward, bounding the gate in one leap, and storming into the yard. It was a suicidal thought that wouldn't solve anything, except to quiet the raging in my head but I stepped forward anyway before catching myself. 'I have to stick to the plan.' Although it was stupid it was the only safe way forward, if there was such a thing when you're chasing a lunatic with a gun.

The main object of my plan stood right in front of me, a rusted wheelbarrow leaning against the side of the barn, gently rotting away in the sun. Rusted and pitted with age it'd obviously seen better days. But it had one big plus; the tire was flat and the metal rung surrounding it was now half dug into the earth. It made a perfect ladder for getting up and onto the metal roof, from where I was guessing there was a perfect view of the yard below.

'Well at least my eyes are still working,' I mused. 'Must be to see that wheelbarrow from the top of the hill.' I realised that I'd spoken out loud and crouched down against the barn wall staring intently at the gate. After a few moments of silence, I rose slowly and tried to work out how best to use the

14

barrow.

'OK, now for the hard part,' I whispered quietly, my calf muscles and back complaining as I stood up. The barrow should be able to take my weight and if it could, it'd give me a good chance of getting up and onto the barn roof. I took off my backpack with a sigh and then my jacket; my t-shirt was plastered to my body underneath. I wrapped the jacket around the lip of the wheel barrow, hoping that it would deaden the sound of metal against brick once I start to climb. It seemed fairly sturdy, wedged up against the wall like it was, but I wouldn't know if was any good until I put my weight on it and started to climb.

Taking a deep breath I slowly raised my foot and placed it gently on the lip of the barrow, twisting it from side to side, to check the purchase and make sure it wouldn't slip, or worse make a terrible racket and give away my position. I settled myself for a brief second and began to rise. My muscles ached with the effort, made doubly hard by the angle that I was trying to climb. I couldn't get any grip on the wall until I was nearly on top of the barrow, so at this stage I was relying on my strength to get me up. Slowly, with a lot of shaking limbs, red cheeks, pursed lips and whistling breath, I rose to a standing position, my arms stretching out slowly across the warm red brick like the legs of a spider carefully feeling their way.

Eventually, my head and shoulders passed over the edge of the barn roof and I stood precariously on top of the barrow, as still as a statue on its plinth. I spread out my arms like a preacher at his pulpit, preparing to start a sermon and took a moment to catch my breath. Looking out over the rooftops of the farmyard, I could see the rolling fields and soft hills of summer. In the middle distance I could see the rooftops of the town I'd raced away from only that morning. I'd lived a lifetime in just a few hours. A gentle breeze whispered through my hair and birdsong filled the sky. If I wasn't in so much danger, I could almost enjoy this moment, stood there precariously over the edge.

'OK what now, Dan? Are you just going to stand there and get a tan or are you going to get up onto the roof and see if he's there like you hoped?' my dad asked curtly.

'I'm going, just give me a minute.' Somehow I had to get up onto the roof. Simple, except it had to be done quietly. Slowly I began to move my torso forward, falling gently to bow to the sun and the sky, my fingers searching blindly on either side of me, feeling the warm rough surface of the roof as they went along.

In one fairly fluid motion I managed to lay on my stomach, my legs remaining at right angles to me, perched over the side of the roof like some naughty school boy waiting for the cane. If only he could see me now, he could shoot me in the rear and walk away. I lay my forehead on the uneven surface, feeling the warmth radiating off the metal and into the skin of my brow.

'Perhaps I'll just stay like this,' I whispered to the roof. An image of the gun floated to the surface of my brain, quickly accompanied by one of blood, rich and dark red slowly spreading across the pavement.

'I never knew a body could hold so much blood,' I sighed.

I rolled over onto my side, my backpack stopping me from getting onto my back and slowly shuffled my way onto the roof. Twisting around, I could see the farmyard below covered in sheds, and old bits of rusting machinery. In the left-hand corner was the back of the farm house, the windows had twee blue and white checked curtains and one sported a porcelain egg basket in the shape of a hen.

Then I saw it, a quick flash of blue I wouldn't have noticed it if I hadn't moved closer to the edge of the roof. He was hidden in the gap between the edge of the farm house and the start of the hay loft, skulking in the shadows like a cold eyed moray eel waiting to strike as soon as its prey came too close. From where he was, he'd have a perfect view of the old red gate, a perfect shot if I'd been stupid enough to come charging in that way. For the first time, I'd got him properly in my sights, but I was unsure of what to do. I didn't have a gun and I was sure a cold hard stare wasn't going to make him drop down dead on the spot.

As I sat there and stared at his hiding place I thought I

could almost hear his shallow breathing as he crouched in the shadows trying to blend in with the walls.

'Why don't you just run, why are you waiting?' I whispered.

The longer he stayed, the better chance I had of getting to him and the better chance of him being caught. Then it hit me; he was afraid of me! That's why he didn't just run away as fast as he could. God knew he'd had enough chances to get away. He was afraid of what I would do. If I didn't carry on chasing him, I would simply go to the police and then it's a man hunt. This way, it's just me and him, a game of cat and mouse. But who's the cat and who's the mouse?

'But why not just shoot me when you have the chance, Bluecoat; what are you waiting for?'

Realising that he wasn't going anywhere soon gave me some relief. I could relax for a short while and get my breath back. My body rushed to agree with me as I rolled back onto my side with a sigh. The bumpy corrugated roof didn't make the best of beds but I didn't care. I needed to rest and try and get my mind into some sort of order. I didn't know if I could let my brain face what happened that morning just yet. All I could see was a brilliant blue sky with a single, fluffy white cloud intruding on perfection; my mind was at peace for the first time in ages. Then I remembered seeing my dad's wedding ring rolling away from his body, a smudge of rich red blood clinging to it. It's strange how things can turn on the most mundane of incidents, from relaxed happiness to screaming murder in the blink of an eye or the ricochet of a bullet.

5 - MURDER MOST FOUL

The taxi ride into town was short but in the heat, with all our gear around us and my dad rabbiting on, it felt like an age. It was the first day we'd spent together in ages. Dad was married to his job, which was probably why his marriage to my mum didn't last, something that really didn't seem to upset the good professor at all. He was so fixed on his own interests, which usually centred on stuff that happened a thousand years ago, that he often didn't know what day of the week it was. He spent most of his time at the university or at ancient sites digging deep into the past. It'd been a while since we'd last been together and I'd forgotten how irritating he could be.

'Now, remember, Danny, you're going to have to have your wits about you today. We're going proper bouldering on some really difficult rocks, so pay attention to me and watch what I do,' he lectured. He was preaching like a vicar in his Sunday pulpit, clearly on a roll and forgetting that he was in a taxi with his son, imagining instead his lecture room full of eager students hanging on his every word. To them, he was the great professor Rochester, renowned historian and all round know-it-all. To me, in the close confines of the taxi, bumping over sleeping policemen and drawing in all the heat of the day he was just Dad. Annoying, droning, boring Dad.

We'd decided to go into town first, then take a trip out onto the moors. Bouldering was our intended activity. A strange pastime for an ancient history professor, but its amazing fun. You climb large smooth boulders, small cliff faces and the like, without ropes or safety harnesses. Totally crazy when you really think about it, but something my dad loved and thought was good for me too. When I was younger, he wouldn't have let me cross the road by myself, but the chance of breaking a limb or doing serious damage while participating in an extreme sport seemed perfectly fine to him. I could never figure him out. Dad got into the sport when my uncle Michael, all round nut job and black sheep of the family, took him on an adventure weekend instead of a stag night. Since then he was hooked, and I quickly found out it was a good way to spend time with him without having to listen to him drone on about some piece of pottery that had been buried in the earth since Jesus was a boy.

'Did you hear what I said, Dan?'

'Yes, pay attention to you, right?'

He narrowed his eyelids and looked down at me from over his nose, not a bad feat considering he was sitting down in the back of a tiny, rickety old cab. 'You were listening to me, weren't you, Dan?' he said, in that quiet voice he used when he was annoyed.

'Of course I was. I just don't see why we have to go into town first.'

He unwrinkled his face and gave a sigh. 'I told you; I need to see someone about a piece of business first. It won't take long, then we can get onto the moors.'

It was always best to change the subject on him when he was annoyed, that quickly got him back on track.

He continued to drone on about his climbing exploits as I sank back slowly into my soft, worn seat, letting the heat inside the taxi and his constant drawl slowly seep over me. The bright day rattled past as we shunted and shook down the road, slowing through road works and wheezing to a slow, exhausted stop at every set of traffic lights. The images outside my window became less focused as the woolly heat clothed itself around my head, easing into my bones and pulling down my eyelids.

I saw a flash of straw coloured hair first, then smelt the lingering promise of expensive perfume, jasmine and bergamot, as it slowly caressed my cheeks and encircled me. She was stunning, standing there in my memory. But then I always knew that. Soft grey eyes and full red lips sitting inside a perfect, oval face, clothed in creamy skin and dotted with a scattering of freckles. Abby had a way about her that drew you in from the moment you met her. She had a welcoming smile and honest expression you could easily warm to. But this hid a will of steel and a determination to match. That had always been our problem; on the surface we were a perfect couple. We shared a lot of the same tastes in music, books, art and the like. But more often than not we could be like two tectonic plates rubbing against each other and when that happened – look out. We'd known each other since we were kids, and had practically grown up together. Our dads had been the best of friends for years; hers was an archaeologist while mine was a professor of ancient history. They were two peas in a very boring pod.

Because we'd been thrust together so much over the years, I guess we were bound to end up as boyfriend and girlfriend. I say that, but I did have to wear her down a bit beforehand. Our getting together was no surprise to anyone. Well, anyone who gave a damn, which was really just her mum. Despite the frequent grumbles, we'd been pretty solid ever since, until her dad had died that is.

They found him slumped over his desk in his office. He often worked late, so no one really noticed until his first appointment the next morning. Everyone thought he'd had a heart attack. He was a workaholic who didn't really look after himself, so it was no surprise. Abby took the news badly. Her mum had never been well and the loss of the absent professor's income meant that the hired help disappeared quickly, so Abby took it upon herself to look after her mum. She was so focused that she refused to go out of the house, or even leave her mum's side unless she really had to. I think she even slept beside her.

Things didn't improve after the funeral and life got

back to normal for everyone else. Her brother, Clive, was no help. He left as soon as he could, saying he had business to attend to. Abby was on her own after that. I tried to help out whenever I could, but you can only really help someone who wants to be helped. Things came to a head between us when I arranged a surprise trip to the cinema. Nothing fancy just a flick and a burger. I even arranged for my dad to look after her mum.

Abby went ballistic when she found out about my surprise. She accused me of not caring and not understanding what she was going through. I was initially taken aback by her reaction but quickly became furious at how self-centred she was being. We had a blazing row in front of my confused and embarrassed father. I guess calling her a crazy witch didn't help. I stormed out of the house and that was that. I'd stayed on at school to finish my A levels, while Abby had left and got a job. Even my mum passing away hadn't helped us patch things up. I'd thought about phoning her but she's got a stubborn streak a mile wide and probably wouldn't even speak to me. So bouldering with my dad was supposed to be yet another attempt to take my mind off her, as if anything would.

The sound of the taxi wheezing to a halt and my dad clambering over me and the gear, babbling as he went, brought me out of my daydream. The sun beating down on my head and the glare seeping into my eyes as I got out of the taxi helped to wash away my heavy head. Tall standing shadows cowered away in corners, offering little relief to stray dogs or overheated boulder climbers. A heat haze rose in wavy lines off the tarmac, curling under my shirt and nestling in the crook of my neck.

'What was that about mad dogs and Englishmen?' I wondered. The shouts of stall sellers peddling everything from onions to ostrich burgers bounced off the shop windows and mingled with the steady hum of a thousand people going about their weekend shopping. 'Dad, do you think this is such a good idea in this heat?' I asked, as he counted the bags and paid the taxi driver.

'Of course it is, Danny; the moors will be empty and the rocks nice and smooth.'

'Oh joy,' I muttered under my breath, looking up at the fierce sun blazing in the morning sky.

'Look!' he replied in response to my frown. 'It'll be fine, we'll have a great time. I just need to see a man about a dog and then we'll be on our way. Why don't you go and get yourself a cool drink and relax for a while? I won't be long.' With that he turned on his heels and casually began strolling down the street, leaving me standing with the bags at my feet. I looked down at them and sighed.

'Going to see a man about a dog, he never says that.' Dad was always so precise about everything. He loved to tell me what he was doing in every minute, boring detail, so why so vague now?

I looked up, meaning to ask him, but by then he was too far down the road. I watched him casually stopping to look in every other shop window, not something he would normally do, either. He hated shopping in general and window shopping in particular. 'Have a plan for what you want and go and get it,' he'd always say. He didn't really look like a guy in a hurry, but who could understand parents? I sighed heavily again and picked up the back packs. It was then, as I looked around for somewhere to get out of the heat, that I saw him for the first time. It was the flash of blue that caught my eye, brilliant cobalt standing out against the drab grey of the doorway he was standing in. It was the colour and the fact that he was wearing his bright coat zipped up to his neck, a strange thing to do on such a hot day that caught my attention. He skulked in the doorway like some predator cat waiting to pounce. Every now and then he'd jerk forward as if to explode outwards and give chase. I chuckled to myself as I watched.

Suddenly, he darted forward and half walked, half ran away from his hiding place. I watched him go and laughed at the silly, urgent walk he performed as he crossed the street. He was clearly trying to get across as quickly as he could without breaking into a full-on sprint and draw attention to himself. I watched as he reached my side of the street. With his back to me, I could now follow his line of sight and the smile fell from my lips as I realised his prey was my dad. I hoisted the back packs over both shoulders and lurched forward after him. In my haste, I didn't notice the cardboard box left out on the edge of the pavement and went sprawling over it with the back packs dragging me down. I watched him sidle down the street and disappear into an alley between two shops. I hauled myself up off the floor as quickly as I could, grabbed the bags, and set off after him.

Picking up the pace, I reached the alley and stopped, staring desperately into shadows, trying to make out shapes. It was an old fashioned covered close, the kind that hid everything more than a few paces from the entrance in a blanket of mysterious grey. I blinked hard and tried to see beyond the ominous shade. After a few seconds, I could make out two outlines further down the alley. They merged and changed into a monstrous form as they stepped close to each other, locked in a hot embrace. Writhing and fighting, the shapes became one then separated, standing a few feet apart, shaking and twitching, before merging again in a desperate, deadly battle for survival.

The light in the alley was as dark as dusk and the fighters were too far away for me to be certain of who they were. I stepped tentatively forward to get a better look. The gladiators parted as I took my second tentative step. Suddenly there was a muffled explosion and one of the dark shapes reeled backwards, crashing off the wall and crumpling to the ground.

A chuckle bubbled up through my throat and parted my lips as I saw the injured shape grapple with the wall and pull itself up like some pathetic drunk. As the shape staggered to its full height I could see something dripping from its body and I realized whoever this was had been shot.

'Dad?'

The second shape had been standing there quietly watching its opponent stagger and bleed. Suddenly, it turned its head in response to my voice. It lurched quickly forward as I took a step back. I could see it hesitate, even in the gloom, and then it turned and ran further down the alley.

I turned to watch the injured monster lurch towards me as the killer rushed away. Like some hungry zombie

23

reaching for its prey, it stretched out its hand as it approached. 'Danny?' it said quietly as it dragged its carcass towards the light.

I froze as a shiver went through me and my mind went blank. The shape was my dad.

The walls of the alley closed in as the creature emerged from the deeper shadows and my worst fears became true. I had to go to him, to help him, to try to save his life. But my feet were frozen to the floor and my mind refused to accept what was happening.

'Danny, please,' the monster whispered, but the words didn't seem to seep in. I knew I had to move, that every second was crucial now. That's what they tell you when you're watching the paramedics on TV. The first ten minutes are crucial, perhaps the difference between life and death. You have to act fast, deal with the patient, identify the problem and try to stop the bleeding. But I wasn't a paramedic and this wasn't a TV show, this was real.

'Danny, please help me.'

'Dad!' I squeaked. 'Dad, what have you done?'

'Help me, Danny.' he gasped, getting closer and closer.

I could see the blood dripping to the floor as he staggered closer to me. It seeped over his hands as they clutched to his stomach. In this light, it looked dark and sinister but I knew that it would turn bright red the moment we emerged from the alley's mouth. It was the blood that unfroze my mind and my feet. I rushed forward and grabbed him just as he was about to fall.

We staggered back into the deeper gloom then crumpled to the floor and lay there in an undignified heap. I cradled his head in my arms and looked down on a face full of confusion and pain. He looked beyond me for a second, then straight into my eyes.

'I've been shot. They shot me, Danny. He had a gun.'

'Yeah, Dad, he was armed, it was a gun, you've been shot, please don't talk, you'll make it worse.'

'Arm, Dan, right arm,' he whispered.

'What? No, don't talk, Dad, it'll be all right, just don't talk. We have to get you to a doctor.' I looked around desperately, not knowing what to do, not believing that this was real, hoping against hope that it was some sick practical joke. 'We have to get you up, we have to get you to a doctor.' I grabbed him as gently as I could and began hauling him to his feet, but he was too heavy and we slipped back to the ground. I remember crying and hearing my dad gasping and gulping for breath. I remember him looking deep into my eyes and smiling. I remember his left arm falling away from him and hitting the floor. His wedding ring rattling loose and rolling along the ground. A smudge of blood caressed its side, alternatively turning bright then dark red as the ring rolled in and out of spars of sunlight. I remember leaning my dad's body against the side of a bin we'd fallen next too and watching as it slid down the side and disappeared. I should have phoned an ambulance and the police. But a small voice inside my head had already started speaking to me. It had only said one thing, but it had been enough. It had said he was getting away.

The blood roared between my ears, my stomach lurched and I gagged in a desperate attempt to keep my breakfast inside me. I spat great globs of spit onto the ground and shook my head to clear it. All thoughts of my dad and calling the police had gone. All I could think about was the guy in the blue coat and the fact that he was getting away. All I heard was the steady drumming of my heart. In that instant I knew what I had to do. I began to chase after him and was running before I reached the end of the street.

6 - I'VE GOT A BRAND NEW COMBINE HARVESTER

It all seemed like a dream. As I lay on the roof of the barn with the sun warming my face and the birds singing in chorus around me, I could almost believe it was a nightmare, but that wasn't true. It was real, and it had all happened over the past few hours. My dad had been shot and I had watched as his blood gently rolled down the pavement and all hell broke loose around me. Even worse, I was now as guilty as Bluecoat; I'd left the scene of a crime. They would be hunting for me too, another fugitive from justice. By now I was sure they'd discovered my dad's body and our gear and knew who he was. They probably knew that someone had been with him too. If they were really clever, they'd know that someone's name by now. And if they knew who I was, they'd be asking some very searching questions about why I'd left my dad's body. Then it struck me that they may even believe I was involved in his murder. That, somehow, Bluecoat and I were partners and we'd planned it all.

Any thoughts I had of letting him go and going straight to the police instead were finished. I had to catch him and get him to confess to his crime; only then would I be in the clear. The only problem was I had to catch him and try not to get myself killed in the process. That was going to be hard.

It's amazing how time can speed up or slow down depending on what you're doing and how you feel. Sometimes, a minute can seem like an hour while at other times an hour can pass as quickly as a minute. I'd processed all these thoughts and cruel reminiscences while catching my breath on the roof of that barn. Everything had taken no more than a couple of minutes and yet it seemed to me like an hour. An hour during which he could have made good his escape. Somehow I knew he hadn't. I knew he would still be there lurking in the shadows, watching and waiting for his moment. He was as scared of me as I was of him and he needed to know where I was just as much as I needed to keep tabs on him. For the first time that day, I had my eyes on him but he didn't know where I was; something was finally going in my favour. I rolled gently over onto my stomach and peered over the edge of the roof. The country scene hadn't changed in the slightest and he was still there waiting in the shadows as I knew he would be.

I lay back and pondered my next move, which basically consisted of jumping down into the yard screaming and charging as I went. Now I was up here, I realised it was a bit higher than I'd originally thought from the other side. I'd be able to jump down, but I might get winded – or worse – in the process. I wasn't keen on the alternatives however – wait where I was until he made a mistake, or find some other way into the yard. I could try jumping down the other side and walking all the way around the far side of the farm, but that would take time and I'd lose sight of him, something I didn't want to do. I was bored with waiting as well, if I was being honest. Now that I had got my breath back, I wanted to get on and get this thing over with. I was sick of chasing him and sick of the hurt. I was sick of not knowing where my dad had been taken and totally sick of Bluecoat shooting at me. I moved closer to the edge and grabbed the lip of the corrugated roof with my left hand. That was when the world tilted on its axis yet again.

The section of roof I'd grabbed hold of was pitted and rusted with age. The weight of my body as I got ready to jump was too much and it snapped off in my hand, totally unbalancing me and sending me over the edge. In my panic I grabbed onto the roof with my right hand and cart wheeled over the side, my backpack falling past me and hitting the ground with a thud. Although I lost my grip as the weight of my body arched and fell into the yard, it did slow me down and I was able to drop onto the floor and avoid serious injury. That couldn't be said for the roof. A large section broke off with an almighty snap and fell with a clatter beside me.

I staggered upwards off the ground and stared down at the offending piece of roof as it rocked to a stop in a pool of its own rust. For a split second, I forgot where I was as I followed the blood red swirls and shapes that encircled the metal corpse. They wouldn't turn brighter in the sun, not like my dad's had. They wouldn't have a chalk outline surround them or be photographed a million different ways. The wind went out of me as I imagined all those police officers busying around my dad's body. No longer a person, just a murder victim, a case needing to be solved.

I sighed for the millionth time that day and looked up into the cold, grey eyes of Bluecoat. Everything fell into the background. All I could see was his haggard face. All I could hear was my steady calm breathing going slowly in and out. The tension of the fall drained away from me while I stood there facing him across the yard. I'd always known this was how it was going to end; how could it finish any other way?

He looked as exhausted as I felt. His eyes had a haunted, scared look about them. Like a fox that had been chased by hounds. My relentless chasing had done all this to him. I was pleased about that. Seeing him standing in front of me, looking so pathetic, made me realize he wasn't the monster I thought I'd been chasing. He was capable of doing terrible things, but he was just a man.

'Well?' I said, with a casual shrug of my shoulders.

He continued to stare at me as he slowly raised his right hand and levelled the gun at a spot between my eyes.

'Go on then coward!' Strangely enough, I didn't feel frightened at the prospect of imminent death. The calm that washed over me when I first laid eyes on him was still in place. I knew this was how it was supposed to end. It was inevitable if you were chasing a bloke with a gun.

Suddenly, he dropped his arm, turned on his heels and ran out of the yard. It took me a moment to realize what had just happened. I stared at the space he had just vacated, then laughter exploded out of me. I was still alive. The coward didn't have the courage to shoot me in cold blood while I stood there staring at him. Pity he hadn't felt the same way about my dad. I stood in the middle of the yard and let out a long, sigh. Tilting my head back, I looked up at the beautiful blue sky. I didn't feel any real urgency to chase after him now. He wasn't going anywhere I couldn't follow and I deserved a brief moment to enjoy the sun. A single white cloud still hung in the air above the farmyard but nothing else disturbed my vision of the brilliant blue dome that stretched over the day. I felt empowered. I'd faced him down. How many times had he had the opportunity to finish me off? Every time he'd failed, I'd become more certain that I could take him. That I could get justice for my dad.

It was the urgent, angry shouts that brought me out of my thoughts. I knew at once that something different was happening. Someone was playing a new game. I ran around the side of the main barn and came out onto the front of the farm just in time to see Bluecoat dive into the driver's side of an old jeep. I stood there and watched as he sped away, the tires spinning and spewing clouds of dust and grit into the air. My heart sank as the jeep quickly wobbled down the country road. I could follow him on foot to the ends of the earth but if he was in a car, I was stumped. The confidence I felt only a few moments ago evaporated like steam. He was gone, I'd failed. Justice wouldn't be done, my dad's death wouldn't be avenged.

'Who the hell are you?'

I stepped back and looked up into the furious eyes and red face standing in front of me.

'He's taken my bloody jeep, did you see him? Who the hell is he and who are you?'

I stood there dumbstruck for a moment as the man ranted in front of me. He was clad in a red checked shirt, brown cord trousers and green wellies. He couldn't be anything other than a farmer and an angry one at that.

'Sorry,' was all I could say as I stared at him, the dust gently spiralling down around us.

'He's taken my car! We need to call the police.' With that he quickly turned away and walked towards the farm house, raising his hands above his head as he went and hurling torrents of abuse and accusations into the warm air.

I turned away from him and noticed that the jeep had stopped a few hundred metres further down the road. A load of cows had temporarily blocked its path. 'Yes!' I hissed. There was still a chance. Looking beyond the jeep, I noticed that the winding country road meandered down the hill and took its time gently curving away to my left. It eventually headed back in the direction of the farm, only this time on the other side of a large field full of cows. If I could somehow get across that field I might have a chance of meeting the jeep as it made its way to the other side. But how on earth was I going to do that?

Then I saw it, parked at the far end of the row of farm buildings, sitting there like a squat green and yellow crab. I could hear it gently humming, a deep throaty sound reverberating across the yard. It was inviting me to climb up, to take a chance and take a ride. I bit my lip and looked around not sure what to do. I couldn't see anything else I could use to get me across the field. The farmer had stopped a few metres away. He had his head down clearly concentrating on pushing the buttons of the phone cradled in his hand. There was nothing else for it. The beast's glass cab winked at me as I made my decision and moved towards it. This was the opportunity I needed but I had no idea how I was going to drive a combine harvester.

I reached the beast and raced up the metal steps. Jumping across the small platform I dived into the cab and scrambled over the passenger seat and sat down behind the large black steering wheel. The cab was spacious and decked with all the latest gear. A TV hung from the roof and a small yellow joy stick stuck out from a bank of flashing controls on my right side. The jet black steering wheel looked out over the front of the combine and despite the fact that it sat behind a vicious looking set of blades, the cab gave me a great view of the surrounding countryside.

I gently took hold of the steering wheel, feeling the powerful engine vibrate through the black plastic.

'How the hell do I get this thing moving?' I asked the air. There didn't appear to be a hand brake of any kind, just the yellow joystick and two pedals beneath the steering wheel. I'd had a few lessons with my dad in his car so I kind of knew how it should work but this was a completely different animal to a Skoda. I knew I was just going to have to try something or be stuck here forever as Bluecoat made good his escape. 'OK let's go for it.'

I guessed the yellow thing has something to do with it so I grabbed hold and began pressing buttons. The enormous blades at the front of the cab began to turn slowly, making menacing ringing sounds as they went. 'Oh Christ, what have I done now!'

I let go of the joystick and grabbed the steering wheel hard. I hovered my foot over what I hoped was the accelerator pedal and prepared myself for whatever came next. A sudden banging on the window made me jump out of my seat. I released my grip on the steering wheel as the window on the passenger side door rattled inwards with the force of the blow. Turning towards the door I was met with a pair of piercing red eyes staring out at me from a beetroot coloured face that was pressed flat against the window.

'Get out!' he hissed.

I looked at him, hesitating for a moment.

'Get out now, boy, or by God, I'll do you some damage.' His checks puffed out as he spat the words. Spit and phlegm running out of his mouth and sliding in a lazy stream down the side of the glass.

He reached out and began pulling at the cab door. Somehow the catch had fallen as he banged on the window and I was now locked in the cab with him ranting on the other side.

'I'm really sorry, I promise to bring it back as soon as I'm finished with it,' was all I could say in a squeaky voice, I wasn't even sure he could hear. I shakily turned my head away from the irate farmer and tried to focus on the road in front of me. He was getting away, I could feel it.

'For God's sake get out, you'll kill yourself!'

'You know this is madness, Danny.'

I started at the sound of my name and turned my head back to the farmer. 'What did you say?'

'This is madness, you'll never get away with it, come out now and I might even let you leave with both your legs,' he hissed, once again sending spit across the window.

For a moment I was sure it had been my dad who'd spoken. He would never have wanted me to do this. I was going way beyond what he would have thought of a normal rational behaviour. Then again he wouldn't have started the chase in the first place. If it had been me who'd been shot he would have gone to the police before my blood had seeped into the pavement.

'Come on boy, let me in, this is just insane. What do you hope to achieve?'

Good question, what *did* I hope to achieve? All this would probably lead to was the inside of a prison cell. I began to lean towards the door. Maybe I should stop what I was doing. My dad was right, this was madness, chasing a murderer across the countryside and nicking a combine harvester in the process. I leant further forward towards the glass door.

'That's right boy, you know you're doing the right thing, you can't drive this thing, you'll end up dead in a ditch.'

I slowly started to raise my hand to reach out and unlock the door when I saw my dad's ring once again, rolling across the pavement with a smudge of blood on the edge. I hesitated there with my hand halfway towards the door. He'd done that. He'd opened up that wound. He caused blood to fall onto the pavement and I couldn't let him get away with it.

I turned my head away from the farmer, set my hands firmly on the steering wheel and slowly depressed the accelerator. The engine's noise grew steadily as the beast began to slowly pick up speed.

'You'd better jump or hang on for dear life, I don't

care which,' I yelled through the glass. I stole a glance and saw him standing there with a blank expression on his face. He looked around and without another word, turned and jumped off the side. From my lofty perch I had a great view of the road slowly coming to meet me. I could see that there wasn't a car coming either way, which was a stroke of luck, considering I was going to have to swerve this thing hard right. But I was picking up too much speed. Looking down to make sure the pedal was still there, I pressed my foot hard on what I hoped was the break. The beast came to an abrupt stop and I was launched forward over the steering wheel and into the glass beyond. My head connected with the window with a crack and my ribs groaned as they crunched into the wheel. I stopped myself from falling between the wheel and the window by clamping my sweaty hands against the glass, screeching to a halt with my face pressed against the windscreen. Shaking my head to clear it, I hauled myself up and fell back into the driver's seat.

I knew I couldn't linger for long. The farmer would be at me again if he thought I was in trouble, but I just needed a moment to get my breath back and clear my head.

'What are you doing, Danny? This is no way to behave.' I opened my eyes with a start, half expecting him to be sat in the seat next to me.

'I can't, Dad, he's not going to get away with what he's done.' I knew it was madness speaking to the air but I had to convince him, or his ghost, that this had to play itself out. He just wasn't going to get away with it, no matter how many combines I needed to steal.

I waited to see if there was any kind of reply but it looked like he was going to remain silent for the time being. I settled back into the driver's seat and gently pressed the accelerator.

7 - Mad cows

I took my time turning the combine onto the main road. I had to direct the huge blades between the verges on both sides, something that was going to have to be done slowly and with as much precision as possible. I turned the large black wheel and tried to edge the machine into the narrow country road. Despite the blades at the front churning up clods of grass and earth, I somehow managed to get the combine onto the road without a hitch. Not bad for a first attempt. That was the easy part; I had get it down the road and turn hard left, through a gate, and into the field beyond. The cows had all strolled into the field by this time and I could see the jeep making its merry way along the lane. It had reached the brow of the hill and was following the arc of the road around the top of the field.

Taking a deep breath, I tried to gauge the point at which I needed to turn and then let the combine rattle down the road. As I approached the gate, I turned the wheel hard left just before the gate post disappeared from view under the combine's blades. I was aiming for a gap between two fence posts but it was made harder by the angle I was approaching from. The beast suddenly jolted into the air as the large left front tire smashed into a post. I was thrown forward once again but was ready for it this time and braced myself against the steering wheel. The combine smacked down with a bang and bounced right as the post disappeared under the beast's belly, scraping and scratching as it went.

Righting itself with a deafening thud, we exploded through the gap and made our way into the field. Cows, whose only worry up until now was where to go to get the best clumps of grass, were suddenly faced with a roaring, screeching mechanical monster bounding and rattling into their field. I laughed as I saw a crowd of black and white steaks scrambling in all directions, desperately trying to get away from the furious beast and its killer blades. Despite the ridiculous scene of terrified cows scrambling away, I knew that hitting one of them wouldn't only be fatal for the animal, it might do untold damaged to the combine and to my chances of getting Bluecoat. Desperately weaving between terrified cattle, I somehow managed to avoid gobbling them up with the combine's blades. But I wasn't able to avoid them all together. One or two bounced off a wheel or careened away off the side of the machine as it rattled through the field. I winced at every jolt and bump and tried not to think of the damage it was doing to an innocent bunch of cows. Just as I thought I'd made it through the worst of my problems, a new one emerged at the far side of the field. I quickly realised that the area been cut in half by a fence to keep the cows in the top field. The second half was a forest of hay bales.

It was the only way I could go, I had no idea how to put the damn thing in reverse so I concentrated on lining up the machine with the gap in the fence. I'd struck lucky once again as the gate was wide open, but it was going to be tight. Aiming for the centre of the gap, I crossed my fingers and hoped for the best.

The beast smashed through the gate with a loud screech as both sides of the rotating blades scraped off the fence posts. But by some miracle I'd managed once again to pilot the monster through an impossible gap. I was through and speeding into the hay field beyond. The machine continued to rattle over the rutted and uneven field, gaining speed as it hit a down slope. Suddenly the hay bales were upon me. I lurched to the right in a desperate attempt to avoid the first one but the field was littered with the honey-coloured mounds, hulking across my path like stationary islands in an empty sea. It was going to be nearly impossible to miss them all.

'Slow down, slow down! Use the brake or you're dead!' I screamed to myself, stepping up out of my seat and depressing the brake as hard as I could, the tendons in my arms and legs stretching as I depressed the pedal and willed the machine to slow down.

Despite my attempts, the harvester continued to trundle forward. I weaved it to the left then the right from my standing position, silent hay beasts flashing past me as we rushed down the field. I missed the next bale by a whisker but then my luck ran out. A bale hit the side of the rotor blades, sending a heavy cloud of gold coloured straw high up into the air. The machine lurched forward and I was propelled over the steering wheel once again, my face hitting the window for a second time. Panic overcame me as I realised the machine was now running free and it was only seconds before we smashed into another bale. My hands flailed against the glass, sweaty palms rubbing up and down the window as I tried to get a grip and haul myself up. Even in my panic I could feel the steering wheel slowly turning and rubbing over my stomach and legs. The combine was turning in a wide arc to the right and into God knew how many obstacles. The window in front of my face fogged over with my exertions as I tried once again to haul myself up. Suddenly, the tiny grip I had managed to get from my palms gave way and I slid further over the wheel and down the glass, my stomach and legs screaming as the large wheel dug into them. The combine lurched to the left as it caught the edge of another bale. That was enough to jolt my legs over the wheel. I was now laying in between the steering column and the front window with a front row view as the combine headed straight to a monster bale lying in its path.

'Get up, Danny, you have to get up and steer this thing to safety,' my dad's calm voice whispered to me from a space in between my ears.

'Do you think?' I huffed, sending spittle against the glass. I was lying on my side with my face against the window. The world flashing before me was full of honey coloured straw, green toned grasses and soft brown earth. The only way I could move was by trying to push myself up from underneath. There was no way I could turn round and I couldn't get any grip on the glass in front of me.

Realising I had only moments before impact, I pushed my arm underneath me and by scraping it along the floor, I was able to raise my torso. I pressed my right hand against the glass and my butt against the steering column. With a great effort, puffing air out in great bellows and screeching until my face turned scarlet, I was able to haul myself upwards, dragging my head and shoulders along the glass as I went. I expected the combine to smash into a mountain of straw at any moment, sending me racing forward through the glass to my death, but somehow I was able to stumble upwards and out from the gap, exhaling air in one long moan of relief when my body cleared the steering wheel. Grabbing the passenger seat I hauled myself up and spun around towards the wheel. I was out but maybe not soon enough, a bale loomed in front of me like a giant straw iceberg. I grabbed the wheel and lurched the machine to the right, hoping I had just enough time and space to miss the monster. The machine groaned as it careened onto two wheels and sped forward. The world tilted sideways as the sky tried to switch places with the land, the hulking leviathan sliding into view for a split second, a giant solitary monster wading in a sea grass, then, miraculously curving to my left as I desperately tried to steer the combine past it. Straw once more exploded upwards as the large left wheel scraped along the side of the bale, but we avoided a deadly impact by the width of a straw. As the machine sped past, it righted itself with a thud. I quickly sat down and pressed the brake pedal as far as it would go. I needed to stop this thing and now. After a few seconds, the combine shuddered to a halt and stood there shivering. I took a deep breath and exploded air out between my teeth.

'That was too damn close!' I screamed, wiping sweat from my face and staring forward into the sea of bales and a straight clear lane running down to the bottom edge of the field. It was only then that I realised the lane had probably been there all along and would be behind me too if I could be bothered to look. I put my head between my hands and started to laugh. Tears streamed down my face as the laughter grew louder. Long, loud belly laughs burst out from deep inside my gut and my whole body shook with the force as it exploded out of me. I was alive. Once again, I'd beaten the odds and was still alive. I had a few more bruises to add to my collection and the tops of my legs were pretty sore from the pounding they took when I fell over the wheel but I'd got off lightly once again. I must have someone watching over me to survive so many life threatening incidents in just one day. If there was a God, surely he was trying to tell me something.

'Bet he doesn't agree with me stealing the combine though,' I gurgled, the thought helping my laughter grow louder until I leant back in the chair to stop my stomach muscles from cramping up. When the hysterics had died down, I wiped my eyes with my hand and looked out to see where Bluecoat had got to.

'I'd totally forgotten about you in all this excitement,' I chuckled, my eyes following the silver line of the road until I saw the jeep. It was still trundling down the road at a slow, steady pace, but it was a lot closer than I'd hoped it would be, I was going to miss it if I didn't get a move on.

'Now for the really dangerous part.'

I lifted my foot off the brake and waited as the combine started to move slowly forward. This was going to have to be done with careful timing; it wouldn't work if the harvester reached the road too quickly.

I watched the jeep continue to make its steady way down the road and pressed the accelerator a little bit more, guessing that my timing might be off. I didn't want to end up behind the jeep after all this. The harvester was now making its way the cleared lane at pace, rattling and bouncing over the uneven field and sending the odd gull flying into the air. It was at this point that I realised I wasn't going to be able to stop even if I wanted to. There was only one thing for it, brace for impact. The combine reached the end of the field at a death rattling speed. It was either going to smash into the hedge and explode into a fireball of burning, twisted, metal and flesh, or punch a way through and crash into a twisted fireball of burning metal and flesh in the middle of the road.

Just so long as I took him with me, at this point I really didn't care. I chuckled at this thought as the combine reached the end of the field.

I caught a glimpse of the jeep as it reappeared and then disappeared behind the hedgerow, then all my attention was focused on the foliage sitting in front of me. I had a moment to hope no endangered moth was taking a nap in my piece of the wall, then the harvester began to rise and the sky tilted upwards. The earth receded below me and a second of weightlessness rippled through my body as the combine rose up against a small bank sitting in front of the hedgerow. But for once my luck ran out. The harvester's vast weight came back down to earth instantly with a thud, hitting the side of the banking and crashing into the hedgerow. The rotary blades began to chew on hawthorn bushes and wild flowers, sending them spewing into the air. The wheels locked into the bottom of the hedgerow and began sinking into the soft earth. The monster let out an all mighty roar as it sunk deeper into the ground. I'd been pushed forward into the steering wheel once again. But had already braced myself for impact and managed to absorb the shock as we connected with the hedgerow. I fell back into the driver's seat as the harvester began to wail and reached over without thinking and switched off the engine. The beast gave off one more groan then died. The blades stopping the instant the engine was switched off. I watched Bluecoat drive past in the stolen jeep and sighed into the gathering silence. He was getting away.

8 - MAD FARMERS

The first shadow crept up the farmer's leg and slowly onto his back. It wobbled over the ruffles in his checked shirt and blackened the dark sweat stain between his shoulder blades. It eventually reached his shoulders, then curled around his neck. He noticed it as it brushed over his ear and began to crawl across his forehead. Twisting around with a start he took a step back at the sight confronting him.

'Good morning, what a pleasant morning it is,' said the first shadow. The farmer looked at what confronted him with a mixture of disbelief and confusion. Recovering his composure quickly he regained the step he'd given up. 'It's not that bloody good a morning,' he replied, pointing towards the combine as it disappeared across the field. 'Someone's stolen my Jeep and a young hooligan's just nicked my combine. The coppers will be here just as soon as I can get a bloody signal. What the hell do you want anyway, I've no eggs and I don't give a damn about Jesus.' He finished his comments in a high pitched whine then turned away for the shadows and began pushing the buttons on his phone once again.

'Oh, dear me, no, we're not here for eggs and I'm afraid Jesus gave up on us long ago,' chuckled the first shadow.

'We are selling something though, and it's cheap at half the price,' interjected the second shadow.

'What was that you said?' the farmer fumed, turning

40

back to the shadows once again. 'You're bloody selling something? Can't you see I've got a crisis here? I've been robbed. Now bugger off!'

'Like I said, we're selling something today, Mr Farmer,' the second shadow continued, taking a menacing step forward that covered the front of the farmer's shirt in a cold, dark gloom. 'We're selling life; would you like to buy some?'

The farmer took an uncertain step backwards once again. 'What do you mean?' he asked in a quieter voice.

'Like my wonderful colleague just said, my rosy cheeked friend, we're selling life, but it's a one off take it or leave it deal, buy now because it's gone tomorrow. If I were you, I'd snap at the chance,' replied the first shadow happily.

'You're off your rocker, how can you sell me something I've already got? What's this all about, have you two escaped from the funny farm or something?'

'Whoooo, funny farm, very droll, l love it. It's always good to keep a sense of humour in a crisis, I always say, and this is a real crisis,' droned the first shadow.

'I know that, you bloody idiot, and you're making it worse, so please go away.'

'Oh, dear me, no, I'm not talking about the naughty little boys stealing your toys, Mr Farmer. I mean right here, right now. We're your crisis and you better deal with us quickly. So please answer my colleague's question; do you want to buy a little bit of life or not? I strongly suggest you take a minute to think about this; you know, your answer could have grave consequences for you.'

The farmer took another uncertain step backwards, his mobile forgotten, senses alert. There was something wrong with these people, all his instincts were screaming this at him. But he was a stubborn and somewhat stupid victim. 'Like I said, I'm not interested in buying or selling so please go away. This is my property and you're trespassing.'

'Oh, that's a real shame,' replied the second shadow, stepping forward to engulf the farmer in darkness.

'Hey, hang on, you, what the hell do you think you're doing? Get away from me.' The farmer's protests were in vain, he'd given his answer and the shadows rarely gave a second chance. His shouting was stopped short as bright blood flooded from the fresh wound opened in his throat. He staggered back clutching his throat in desperation.

'Now mind you don't get any on your clothes,' the first shadow warned.

'Of course I will, I'm always careful,' replied the second shadow.

The protesting farmer finally ended his days as a corpse hidden behind a rusted old tractor at the back of a barn with a bit of the roof missing. The shadows however continued on their merry way, without a spot of blood on their fine clothing.

9 - THE CASTLE ON THE COAST

I left the combine to its bushy grave and clambered out onto the main road. To my amazement no other cars had travelled down it since I'd smashed into the hedge-row. From the lower angle of the road you couldn't see much of the carcass and most drivers would simply think the farmer had parked it too close to the edge of the field. I hauled my rucksack over my shoulder and trudged down the road in a futile effort to keep up with Bluecoat. After a mile or so I came upon a bus stop. Figuring it would be better to get the bus rather than walk to wherever I was going I leant against the side of the shelter and waited. The sun was high in the sky by now and to my amazement I realised it was only around lunchtime. I'd been chasing him for so long it seemed like a life time. But it had only been a few hours and I'd only trav-elled a few miles. Not the thousands my feet were telling me I'd walked. I sighed and wondered where he was now. Prob-ably laughing his ass off and listening to tunes on his stolen car's radio. After a few more quiet minutes the bus came trundling down the road. I stepped on and paid my fare, then sat down with another sigh. The seat felt warm and soft after my escapades across the countryside. It was good to just sit and wallow for a while. I stared out at the passing landscape and wondered again where he was. Then I saw the squat outline of the castle through the dirty brown windows of the bus and knew exactly where he'd gone.

'Yes!' I hissed to myself.

'Are you alright dear?' a kindly looking old lady asked from the seat opposite.

'Yes, I'm fine thanks. Just seen the football score on my phone, Liverpool scored,' I lied. My phone was still in my backpack, out of charge as usual.

'Oh they are marvellous things aren't they? My grandson has one too. If you don't mind me saying you look a bit dishevelled, is everything alright?'

'Oh, yeah everything's fine, I've been out hiking and climbing through a few hedges and stuff. It was harder than I thought.'

'Here, take this,' she said, holding out a wipe. 'My Douglas swears by them. That's my eldest. He's a mechanic and uses these to get the grease off his hands.'

'Thanks,' I said, taking the wipe and cleaning my hands and face. Wiping away a bit of my dad's dried blood from my hands. Amazingly I hadn't got any on my clothes. The lemon smell was refreshing and, once I'd finished, I felt better than I had all morning.'

'That's better,' the old lady said with a nod. 'So is that you off home now?'

'No I need to go to the castle, then home.'

'Oh, that's a lovely place. Haven't been there in a while though. Hope you enjoy it?'

'Thanks, I'm sure I will. I'm hoping to meet someone there.'

'My Stan and I, that's my husband, use to go there a lot before he died. The cakes are marvellous, you should try them when you're there.'

'Thanks I will.'

'At least you're avoiding the town. I heard there was a bit of a thing this morning.'

My heart sank at her words.

'Really?' I said, trying to sound as casual as possible.'

'Yes, someone's been shot. I've not heard anything else but apparently it was some tourist who got robbed and things went wrong. It sounds terrible.'

'Yes, that does sound terrible,' I replied. My heart starting to beat quicker inside my chest.

'You're not safe in the streets these days, even in broad daylight. What is the world coming to?'

'It's a real worry,' I replied.

'It's the young I worry about. What world will they be living in, in years to come?'

'A good one I hope,' I replied with a thin smile.

'Well I hope that too.'

Just then the castle came looming into view. 'This is my stop,' I said, getting up. 'Thanks for the wipe.'

'Hope you enjoy your visit? Remember to try the cakes.'

'Will do,' I said, stepping off the bus.'

It was only after the bus had disappeared around the bend that I realised I'd left my backpack on the seat next to me.

'Damn!' I hissed. 'What the hell do I do now?' I had no money to get in and it wasn't cheap as I recall. With a sigh I started up the hill.

The castle was set on a low plateau overlooking the sea. To get to the main entrance, you had to follow the curve of the road as it ran around the east side of the walls and met the portcullis entrance guarded by fierce looking gargoyles staring out over the sand dunes and the sea. I mingled easily with the scattering of tourists happily making their way towards the castle gates, some chatting amiably about last night's salmon dinner and the price of entrance to historic sites. A rich mixture of Spanish, Japanese and some Eastern European language I didn't recognize, helped to give the crowd a cosmopolitan feel. It almost seemed normal as we slowly made our way up the road. Then I realized that along with the old lady on the bus, these were the first people I'd seen for a long time who weren't trying to kill me. Even so, I edged my way to the side of the crowd just in case.

As soon as we got to the main entrance, I knew I was in trouble. I'd automatically reached over my shoulder for my back pack but it wasn't there. I was stuck out here with no way of paying to get in.

I walked towards the castle entrance and the admissions office beyond, hoping to get inspiration before I got there. The gatehouse towers loomed above me, two ancient sentinels blocking my path to revenge. The Spanish and Japanese noisily queued to get in while the Brits stood quietly, tutting amongst themselves.

'Now remember, Danny, you're entering the Vale Typping, a narrow road that leads to the great tower. The admissions office here used to be a prison cell,' my dad lectured me from beyond the grave.

'Hello again, long time no see,' I replied under my breath.

He was becoming just as boring in death as he had been in life. I could see him standing there, totally in his element. He loved the castle and tried to visit it as often as he could. He helped Abby's dad out on the digs they conducted in the castle grounds, getting a kick out of that and the fact that it was his castle. Well, I say his, but it was really a distant cousin's. We were very distant relations to the baron, a guy who probably would have walked passed us in the street, but that never stopped Dad from reminding anyone who cared to listen that this was his family's castle. 'The Seat' as he called it. I sighed at the memory of his enthusiasm and love for the place, something I could never share with him no matter how many times he insisted on bringing me along.

The stories he'd tell me as we walked around the outer curtain wall, when I was a child, were great, especially the ones with all the blood and guts. I really liked to hear about what they used to do to prisoners and spies in the dungeon. The story of the rack and the cage were particularly gory, but it got boring really quickly and even more so after you'd heard it for the millionth time. Things only got interesting when Abby was forced to endure these trips as well. Her dad also thought these were educational trips for the youngsters and that they would learn to appreciate them in time. Over the years Abby and I would shrug them off as quickly as we could and go exploring ourselves. This usually meant a trip to the armaments museum located in the west ward, there and the café, of course, when we were older. I figured young love would always blossom over a couple of cokes and a cake. I may have known her since we were little kids but the time we spent on our own around the castle showed me another side to her; a softer, more sensitive side. We didn't even argue as much as we did when we were with our parents.

I liked what I saw and hoped she did too. Eventually I managed to wear her down with my bad stories and terrible jokes. Abby was the prettiest girl in school, when we were younger, and I was the envy of most of the male population of 'The Maggot' as St Margaret's High, my school is lovingly known. Probably because it's the kind of place where maggots thrive. If anything, one or two of the more sporty minded 'studs' couldn't understand how I'd made such a catch. I can hold my own in a game of five-a-side but I'm no sportsman, something they thought was a requirement for going out with Abby. But if you got to know her, then you realize that wasn't the case. She wasn't into the sporty types, she liked the more sensitive types and besides I knew her secret; she had a real weakness for a scone with clotted cream.

The loud blaring of the coach's horn jerked me out of my daydreaming. I hadn't realized I was standing in the middle of the road blocking its path to the car park. I quickly got out of the way and watched as it wheezed by, disappearing around the side of the castle wall to an area reserved for large coaches and buses. Then a spark of an idea struck me as I watched it go. I might not be able to pay to get into the castle but there's more than one way to skin a cat as they say.

I ran after the coach, trying to catch up with it before it got too far in front, hoping to disappear behind its belching backside and mingle amongst the general crowd standing around parked vehicles and screeching horns. I wasn't too sure that the public was allowed around this side of the castle.

A group of drivers huddled together in a tight group of flashing orange embers and hazy, smoky air appeared in front of me as I got around the side of the coach. Luckily they took no notice as I shoved my head into my shoulder and casually sauntered past. This was a touristy place after all and plenty of them got lost around here. I was guessing that none of them was a possible fugitive.

The car park ended all too soon and I was on my own, looking up at the outer wall rising above me, the odd head and arm appearing over its top. Although it was much lower at this side of the castle, I still figured the wall was about ten metres high. Not a cliff face but still dangerous enough for someone who might want to climb up it without a harness. I wasn't too bad at bouldering and I had a good teacher in my dad, but I certainly hadn't tried to climb something that he hadn't checked out before hand and never without him standing at the bottom giving me instructions.

'There's the battery gate just along the path here, Danny. It allowed horse drawn vehicles to access the castle without having to navigate the steep Vale Typping. They were brought to their knees on that road you know.' I did, I could see them there, lathered in sweat, breathing out streams of white steam into the frosty air, noses flaring, eyes bulging as they strained on their harnesses. Iron clad hooves clattering over the cobbles, sending the odd spark flying. Some would try so hard that their heart burst. They'd collapse into their tethers and die on the cold ground. There was a large painting in one of the state rooms that showed this ugly scene. Men gathered around the dead beast, pointing fingers and showing angry faces. None of them cared for the animal, it was the cost that they cared about and the fact that they'd now have to carry the load themselves. I always felt that the painting was at odds with its grand surroundings. Odd looking and menacingly called 'A trip to the glue factory'. I shuddered at the memory of it and hoped that it wasn't still there.

'You're right, Dad, I forgot about the battery gate.' I sauntered over to it, just another tourist who wanted to check out some old gate. I could see the inside of the castle through the lattice work of wooden bars as I approached it. It was set deep into strong sandstone blocks, weathered with age. The cobbled path carried on beyond the gate and up into the castle proper. I was so close but so far. The gate was locked shut and a brief rattling of the bars only got me a strange stare from a guy taking pictures on the other side. I couldn't get in from here.

I continued to walk along the path running parallel with the wall, this time taking more notice of the way the stone blocks bulged and protruded outwards at different sections and heights. I wasn't worried about being spotted by security, now I was away from the prying eyes of the coach drivers. The castle had no CCTV or security system to speak of. I'd been told the current lord of the manor much preferred to spend his money on fast cars and loose women. The path came to an end in front of a large hawthorn bush, overgrown and spreading along the base of the wall. I knew the castle continued beyond this point and was a bit quieter than the rest of the grounds. Being careful not to stumble and fall down the grassy hill, I made my way around the bush. Its supple branches pulled and pushed me along, this time keeping me from falling, the next giving me too much slack and nearly sending me down the slope and into the grassy dunes below. After a bit of huffing and puffing I made it around the bush and arrived in another country.

10 - ANOTHER COUNTRY

It was a country of sand dunes covered in tall lime green grasses whispering to each other in the breeze. It was a country of majestic grey-white seagulls singing high up in the rich blue sky and small red and yellow dots bobbing up and down between the dunes while the odd bark carried along on the wind. Thankfully no blue blobs appeared to spoil the view. The wind, which had only been a quiet hum on the other side of the hawthorn bush, now caressed my face and chased strands of hair across my head. It was an idyllic feeling to stand there in the cool northern breeze but menacing too. Despite the warm day, the wind would freeze my fingers and the noise might cover any warning I would have of someone watching me from above. I might risk life and limb to get up the castle wall only to be met by the police when I got up there. I couldn't worry about that right now though. Even if I did draw attention to myself, I had to risk it, I had to get over that castle wall.

I continued along the base of the wall and began to think of the climb in front of me. I had to be confident, I had to believe that I was going to reach the top. As I watched, its softly undulating surface seemed to breathe in and out; this wasn't some cold lifeless object, it was alive and it had been waiting for me.

'Come on, Danny', it whispered, 'you can do it, and we'll help. Look how we rise and fall here, a perfect spot to start. We're even lower at this point, you'll be up and over in a minute.'

Its caramel-coloured bricks, all weathered and aged, urged me to climb while I stood there and tried to imagine myself reaching over the top. I knew they'd seen everything in their time, I was nothing new. I imagined them seeing another man, in another age, desperately trying to build himself up to do something dangerous. Something so stupid only a desperate soul would contemplate it.

'I'm losing my mind, even the stones are talking to me now.'

I took a deep breath to calm my nerves and looked up to the top of the wall. The point I'd reached was perfect. It was no more than six metres high and there were enough cracks and crevices to give me a fighting chance. There was even a large water spout sticking out near the top. I knew this was the best I was going to get, I might not hurt myself too badly if I slipped. I gently placed one of my hands onto the smooth, weathered surface, feeling the warmth from the stone sink into my palm.

'Three points of contact at all times.'

This was just like any other boulder. Hell this was even easier, it had more places to hold onto. I could practically climb up it like a ladder. I erased all the hurt and heartache of the day from my mind. Only the climb mattered now, I was going to climb easily and get to the top without any effort.

'Three points of contact at all times, Danny.'

'Three points of contact, Dad, got it.'

I looked down for some chalk to rub on my hands, as I'd been taught. There wasn't any, of course. Something else I'd left in my backpack.

'I'll just have to wing it, then.'

Looking down, I spotted one of the large stone blocks jutting out just above my knee. This would be my first step. Placing my foot onto its edge I turned my attention to the rest of the wall. I closed my eyes and rubbed my hands across its surface feeling for the best holds. When I was sure I'd got the best I could find, I grasped them with my fingers and lifted myself up with the tops of my palms, using the foothold to steady myself. This was the start of the climb, some would say the hardest bit. It's too easy here, you can just step off without any danger. It's only your pride you can break at this point. That was why most beginners fail at the start. Their fear overcomes them and they step away before it becomes too serious. It was already far too serious for me. I had a goal that could only be reached well after my climb was finished. This wasn't the beginning, I was already half way through.

Remembering my dad's advice, I hugged the wall and imagined my holds were as big as steps. I kept my three points of contact and reached out methodically with my free hand, searching for the next hold. My mind was blank at this point. I had to be calm and confident, feeling nothing but the stone, thinking about nothing but reaching the top. My body began to ache more quickly than it had on the times I'd tried this before. Then again, I hadn't chased a murderer across the countryside on those occasions. My muscles complained about yet more strain and exertion and I could feel the beginnings of cramp start to set into my calf muscles. I blanked the feelings from my mind as best I could. I had to get up before it got too hard and my body gave up the fight and gravity took over. I was making good progress and finding sound holds as I went when I looked up to see Bluecoat's face appear above the rim of the wall, his eyes boring into my strained, up-turned face. I froze in my tracks, my muscles locking and my fingers boring into the stone. His face stayed as still as a statue for what seemed an eternity, then it faded into the breeze. I let out a sigh and tried to relax as much as I could. It wasn't him, it was just my imagination playing tricks on me. I continued up the wall, returning to my thoughtless regime with ease. Before I knew it my hand struck the large, flat water spout. I was nearly there. I remembered that the spout was no more than a few metres below the top. I took hold of it with a firm grasp and began to haul myself up.

Suddenly pain seared through my hand and I felt warm blood trickle over my fingers. I looked up with a start to see a fat, white gull with jet black eyes attacking my fingers with ferocious intent. It stabbed down again and I let out a gasp as pain lanced through my hand. My grasp on the spout loosened, my weight suddenly shifted and I began to ease away from the wall.

Another jolting stab of pain made me lose my grip on the spout. My hand wheeled away in an arc above my head, spatters of blood flying from it as it went. The momentum caused as it fell behind me forced one of my feet out of the tiny crevice it was clinging to. Suddenly I was hanging by one hand and one foot.

'Three points of contact!' I screamed inside my head.

I could feel my body slowly start to peel itself away from the wall. The fingers and tendons of the hand still clinging to the surface screamed in agony as the pressure on them built. I was only a crumb of stone away from losing my grip entirely and plummeting down to the grassy hill below. I felt the veins in my temple throb with the pressure. My joints shook and my body screamed against yet more punishment. I fought against the momentum with all my strength and determination. I dare not breathe unless my expanding lungs pushed me further away from my precarious position and into empty space.

'Let go, it's not that far,' the wind mumbled across the back of my head with a chuckle. 'You'll hardly feel a thing, and when you reach the bottom you can dust yourself off and start again. There won't be gulls next time.'

I shook my head as much as I dare in order to block out the stupid, imaginary voice rattling around inside. Hearing the wind talk to you was bad enough. It was even worse when you were fighting for your life. Right then, I would have welcomed my dad's imaginary drawl; at least he was human.

With every ounce of strength I could muster, I stopped the momentum in my arm and pulled it forward and up, reaching for the overflow and a safer grip. My hand made contact with a satisfying slap, sending the startled gull into the air. I gripped the spout as firmly as I could and prepared to haul myself back up into a better position. Suddenly, my other hand popped out of its crevice. I was jolted outwards and both my feet gave way. I locked onto the spout as my body swung underneath like a pendulum. My only hold onto life a blood spattered hand. My feet turned to heavy dumbbells pulling me down to the ground. My wrist creaked with the strain and my hand throbbed with the weight. I knew that in a few seconds my grip would go entirely and I would finally take that trip down. I could see it now, a hurling vision of browns, greys and greens as my body was grabbed by gravity and embraced by the warmth earth.

'Reach out with your free hand, Danny. Remember, you have time, as long as you reach out now.'

He was right, it was my only hope. I reached out and caressed the stone with my free hand, gently trying to find a crevice or crack that would give me any kind of purchase. My body had now come to a stop below the spout but the weight in my feet was increasing, my arm and shoulder were screaming and I could feel my fingers begin to loosen. Without any chalk to give them purchase the blood eased beneath them, making my hold slippery and wet.

'Don't let go, Dan, if you let go you'll keep falling forever.'

I tried as best as I could to blank everything out of my mind. I needed to be an empty shell, nothing existed but my grip on the spout and my fingers crawling across the surface of the wall. Rivulets of sweat ran down my back, my muscles seized and my temples pounded with rushing blood and pressure. I dare not reach out with my feet until I had some kind of hold with my other hand. That kind of movement would surely send me spiralling downwards just as quickly as hanging here would. I continued to run my fingers across the bumps and cracks in front of me relying on feel rather than sight to get a hold I could use. My gentle probing found a crack too small then a ledge too thin. I was reaching the end of my strength and beginning to contemplate the ride down to the bottom when my fingers found a decent hold. I locked on with all I was worth and tried to take some of the strain away from my other hand. My body eased its screaming as the weight was distributed more evenly and I was able to start scrambling for footholds. I found a couple surprisingly quickly and rested my weight evenly across my arms and legs, finally able to draw in lung-bursting sacksful of air. My head swam for a moment and blue stars flittered across my closed eyelids but my grip held. The sparks scattered across my dark vision, bumping into one another, leaving spiralling blue trails and disappearing around corners.

After a moment, my head began to clear and the dizziness faded. The gentle breeze I was so worried about now caressed the nape of my neck and dowsed my hot forehead with its cool breath. Even though my head had cleared, I needed a moment to fully recover and to make sure I wasn't going to lose my grip and go tumbling down. I knew I couldn't wait too long, though; my strength was already draining away and I wasn't sure I had enough left to finish the climb. After what seemed an eternity I felt sure enough to open my eyes and see that I wasn't going to fall after all, I was still clinging precariously to cracks and fissures in the wall, not to mention the ancient water spout. Despite my mishaps, I now saw I'd made good progress and was only a few scrambling footholds away from the top, a few more minutes and it was all over. Then the gull landed on my scratched and pitted hand, its feathers gently tickling my skin as it swooped down. It looked at me with black eyes, its head bobbing from side to side as its webbed feet sort purchase on my soft flesh. This wasn't going to happen again. I took in as big a lungful of air as I dare and hissed at the evil bird. The sound sent it wheeling into the air, its wings flapping frantically. Without a second thought for my weary body I pulled myself up using the spout as leverage and began the climb once again. I didn't want to give the monster another chance to come back and fight me. The next few minutes were filled with searching and scrambling hands and shaking and seizing muscles, my hands and feet raking across the ancient surface looking for holds that would finally get me up and over. Suddenly my hand felt the welcome curves of the top of the wall. I took a firm grip and levered myself over the lip, sliding the last few feet on my belly, my hands flailing in front of me and my legs pushing from below. I flopped over the top like a giant fish dropping into a bucket and collapsed in a heap onto the soft grass. I was a deflated body bag, its contents scattered away on the breeze. I couldn't move even if he was standing over me with a gun aimed at my head. My muscles sagged into the ground, all feeling in my legs disappeared and my head suddenly became too heavy to hold up. I could feel my remaining strength seep away like water out of a broken cup. All I could do was concentrate on breathing in and out, letting the lactose dissolve and trying to get as much air into my exhausted body as I could.

'Enough, no more exercise for one day, that has to be my ten thousand paces and then some.' I laughed inside at the thought. Abby had been pretty keen on keeping fit. 'You have to walk at least ten thousand paces a day, Dan, otherwise you'll grow flabby. I don't want a flabby boyfriend.'

That little comment had led to another argument. I wondered what she would think of my fitness regime now. I guess her opinions on keeping fit had been another reason why I'd stuck with the bouldering; every cloud as they say.

After a time, my strength began to return and I was able to sit up and shuffle backwards to lean against the wall. I was now just an everyday tourist taking a break in the sun. Just one who was as weak as a new-born. At least I would be as long as no one saw me when I'd flopped over the wall's lip and collapsed in a heap on the grassy floor. I looked up and realised why no one was rushing forward, to help or arrest me. By sheer chance they'd erected a large display in front of this section of the wall. I was sitting behind it looking at blank brown boards. No doubt the front was full of interesting pictures and information covering the history of the castle. Either way it meant that no one had seen me flopping over the lip of the wall and sitting there gasping for breath. I stood up shakily and brushed myself down. Straightening my hair and making sure my clothes looking presentable. Then, as casually as I could manage I sauntered around to the front of the display. The west ward; a large expanse of deep green grass with the inner wall bordering on the eastern side, opened up in front of me.

'Inner curtain wall, Danny, get it right.'

A large archaeological dig bordered the outer wall on the south side and an ancient bell tower stood sentinel at the south-western tip. This was now called a 'picnic area' but luckily for me, no one was sitting eating their sandwiches and crisps. A few touristy types were clustered around the dig but it was far enough away that no one would have noticed me unless they were looking in that direction.

'Did you know this was the first castle in England to fall to cannon fire, Danny?' I was momentarily distracted from my search by my dad's know-it-all drawl once again sounding in my brain.

'Give it a rest, just for once. OK now what?'

Chuckling, I realized that I hadn't given that question much thought recently. I'd been so intent on getting up the castle wall without breaking my neck I'd forgotten the reason why I did it in the first place. I walked back to the wall and stared down at the way I'd just come. The gull was back in his spot huddled in the middle of the spout, looking out over the coast with a vacant stare.

'You're lucky I'm on a mission, mate, or I'd come down there and grab you for the pot! I bet you'd taste nice in a creamy gull pie. As it is, I've got to see a man about a dog,' or a Bluecoat about a shooting.

11 - A BALL IN THE KING'S HALL

Like most castles in England, my dad's wasn't one but many, each one built on top of the other over hundreds of years. This was what kept him and his cronies so occupied. They got almost apoplectic with excitement when they found a piece of pottery that confirmed their belief, brought about by some other bloke's finding, based on a third dude's guess work, that there used to be a kitchen here when Moses parted the Red Sea and not ten feet further away, as was originally thought.

What was good about the place when I was growing up, apart from Abby, is that it's a real rabbit warren of rooms and halls. You can get lost really quickly, always a good thing when you're trying to avoid the great Professor Rochester. That was why I was certain he was here. It was a great place to find a bolt hole and no one would question why you were hanging around the same spot for hours, you were supposed to do that. I knew he wouldn't be out in the open, though; he'd be inside, hiding behind a 300-year-old chair.

The stinging in my hand as I brushed it through my bedraggled locks reminded me of the encounter with the gull. I looked down to see small pits and scratches now covered the top of my hand. Blood had trickled in jagged lines across the back and into my palm. It was smudged over my finger tips and was drying under my fingernails. I looked like a butcher, but without the bloody apron. My first port of call had to be the bathroom. I needed to wash the blood off my hands, and do something to tidy my hair. 'God I sound like Abby!'

I knew where the toilets were of course, why wouldn't I? They used to be the old stables. Funnily enough, the horse stalls were now the toilets. I don't know what you're meant to take from that about the similarities between humans and horses but it always gave me a chuckle.

I stood up straight, my arms and legs creaking and a moan of pity slipping through my lips. My back popped like an old man's as I stretched and moved about, trying to ease my stiff and sore muscles. With one more click and a snap of my neck just to stop my back feeling lonely I shook off my tiredness and made my way into the main part of the complex.

The toilets were clean and bright and thankfully empty when I reached them without any further incidents with gulls, tourists or gunmen. I went straight to one of the sinks, turned on the tap and began gulping down cold water. I didn't realize how thirsty I was until I saw the gleaming chrome taps and my body started to ache for refreshment. Water splashed over my face and hands as I greedily slurped at the crystal clear stream. I could feel my tired body groan with contentment and my head begin to clear. When I'd drunk my fill, I began to wash the blood off my hands, trying to ignore the stinging it caused. The dried flakes mingled with the cold water and ran in rivulets over my fingers, dripping into the sink and staining the bright white porcelain a pale pink before swirling away. Once my hands were a healthy red I brushed myself down once again and washed my face. After that I was ready to start looking for him.

'Now for the King's Hall, Dad; I bet you'll like that.'

I left the toilet and walked through the inner courtyard and up the hill towards the keep and the buildings beyond. Children ran in crazy circles all around me while chattering groups of strangers excitedly pointed cameras and mobile phones. A mock throne seemed to be a particularly popular photo opportunity. I casually tried to avoid the pointing lenses as I made my way past. The great stone keep stood proudly on the highest point of the castle enclosure like some solitary solider standing guard against time. Just beyond it, there was another series of buildings. They abutted the keep on the eastern side and made up the rest of the main castle complex. Here were apartments, kitchens, salons and the magnificent King's Hall, my dad's favourite bit of the whole complex. This was where I was going to try first.

To get inside, you had to go via the inner ward, a large grassy area just to the side of the keep. It was quite empty when I got there. One solitary workman was unloading bright blue gas canisters from a truck and placing them onto the smooth green lawn, something that was clearly going to get him into trouble if the look on the face of the guard walking towards him had anything to go by. I breezed past him and opened the heavy wooden door that would take me into the state rooms. The second I walked over the threshold I entered yet another world.

The quiet heavy air wrapped its arms around me as I walked in, the large oak door gently closing behind me with a satisfying click. A wizened old attendant looked over from the cloistered corner she'd secreted herself into, smiled and went back to reading her book. The large stateroom opened out in front of me, revealing thick glass cabinets holding expensive dinner sets and large pewter bowls. Grand oil paintings jostled for attention alongside rich oak cupboards that lined up like sentries against the white washed walls.

'That's a *sang de boeuf* vase, Danny, and those are French restoration mahogany chairs.'

I scanned the room quickly, seeing through the exhibits and ignoring my dad's excited commentary. I concentrated on the few tourists casually floating around the space like serene ghosts. Eliminating them one by one as I tried to see into all the nooks and crannies, I suddenly saw a flash of blue around every corner, a red-rimmed eye behind every glass case. He was everywhere and nowhere. He was behind my eyelids. He'd wormed his way into my dreams. For a moment, I wasn't sure what was real and what wasn't. How could he be here and then disappear? Then, as quickly as the panic came, it drained away as calm washed over me; I knew he wasn't in the room. This wouldn't be a good enough hiding place for him. Why go to all the trouble of getting into the place if all you were going to do was hide behind a stuffed polar bear in the first room you came to. He'd be deeper in the bowels of the building, crouched behind a medieval tapestry or something. I didn't know where he was, but I did know he'd be expecting me to chase him. That meant he'd be somewhere with a view, somewhere dramatic, somewhere containing much, much more than Coalport china sets and Anglo-Flemish cupboards.

'There's only one place, then.'

I knew it all along, it was time for a ball. I made my way in a blur through rooms of oak and antiques, my quickening footsteps tapping an insistent beat on honey-coloured floors. Flashes of bright blue continued to give me starts. Each time they proved to be an innocent bystander, or, worse, a member of staff. It looked like bright blue was the colour of their uniform.

After what seemed an age of snaking through mahogany-coloured rooms full to bursting with antique clocks, plates and portraits, I finally reached my destination. The King's Hall opened up in front of me with a flourish. My footsteps now beat a reverential tone as I crossed the threshold into a grand scene of pistol-filled cabinets and rows of silent armour, a wide open space at its centre the only reminder of its true purpose.

'It used to be a place of much feasting and merriment, Danny. Stories of the grand balls once held here and the amount of alcohol consumed by the old Duke are legendary.'

Golden bars of light splashed down from high windows, some of which were transformed into tiny blood red droplets by a large stained glass windows on the far side of the hall. Butter-coloured roof beams drooped down like tears, while the grand picture was completed by the minstrels' gallery sitting high up at the south end of the building, crowned by the famous round rose window full of armorials depicting the lords and ladies of the castle's past.

'Those are Siamese teak "false hammer" beams, Danny, truly impressive.'

I made my way carefully into the centre of the hall, constantly roaming the space with my eyes, expecting to see him at any moment. Reaching the very middle, I paused, waiting for what was to happen next. A scattering of fellow tourists walked past me, eyes gazing everywhere, mouths lolling open as they looked upwards into the vast roof above. Now, just when I needed it the most, I couldn't see a smudge of blue anywhere.

'He's got to be here, he has to be watching. Come on show yourself you bastard.' The words rolled around my tongue and dribbled through my gritted teeth as I waited for something, anything to happen. I felt more frustrated than exposed. I knew he wasn't going to shoot me and was more concerned that I was on a wild goose chase.

'What the hell are you doing here?'

I turned around with a start and met Abby's cool grey eyes and stern, set face. 'What?' was all I could manage?

'What are you doing here, Danny?'

For a moment the question left me confused. What was I doing here? Why had I ended up hunting a murderer in the bowels of a medieval castle? I could have given a million different answers but all would have been wrong. The truth of it was I didn't really know. There was something I just couldn't let go; revenge, anger, frustration, justice, they all played a part but they weren't the real answers. Then it struck me, rising up from deep down inside my gut and exploding into my brain, the truth I'd ignored from the start. I was doing it because I enjoyed it, plain and simple.

'Well, I ...' was all I could manage standing there under the gaze of those eyes.

'Come on, Dan, spit it out; you know you shouldn't be here.'

That shook me out of my lethargy. The real Abby was standing in front of me, just as annoying as always, just as controlling, just as stern.

'What the hell do you mean, I shouldn't be here? It's a public place isn't it, and who are you to tell me where I should and shouldn't be?'

'You know what I mean.' she hissed, moving in close. 'After everything that's gone on, you shouldn't be here.'

I took a step forward and looked straight into the pools of her pale grey eyes. 'Why, Abby? What's gone on?'

'Your dad, Dan,' she sighed.

'What do you know about that?'

'It's all over the news. A man's been shot in the market place.'

'As opposed to the chest, you mean?' I retorted with a giggle.

'You shouldn't be here, she repeated.'

'How do you know? What have you been told?'

'I haven't been told anything, I've only seen what's been on the news. I haven't a clue why you're here of all places, but I do know it's the wrong place to be.'

Her presence, lovely as it was, wasn't what I needed right there and then. She was a distraction, plain and simple. Worse, she was reminding me of that other life. The one that was waiting for me after Bluecoat. The one with all the pain and guilt and questions. God, there were going to be so many questions.

'I have to go, nice to see you again, Abby.'

'What!' She stared at me incredulously. 'What do you mean you have to go? The only place you need to go is the police station.'

She took another step closer to me, until we were just a nose width apart, her eyes wide, her expression set, her familiar perfume enveloping me as she drew closer.

'Babe, you shouldn't be here.' Just like always, she was pushing me towards her point of view by the sheer force of her presence. Her eyes, her face, her body, were all weapons as far as Abby was concerned. All could be used to get her what she wanted, or to break what she didn't. What she wanted right now was my full and undivided attention. I shook my head and took a step back.

'You don't understand. I have to go.' I turned my head to look around the grand hall once again. 'He might be getting away,' I muttered, half to myself.

'Who might be getting away?'

63

Then I saw him, standing bold as you like at the far end of the hall. No longer hiding behind an old chair or the end of a tapestry, just standing there as still as a statue, surrounded by splashes of blood red sunlight, watching me with a small smirk of amusement peppering the corners of his thin, grim mouth.

I took a step towards him, drawing in a breath, getting reading to chase. Abby pulled at my sleeve, as I walked passed her, trying once more to bring me into her world. 'Where the hell are you going? Who's getting away? Don't walk away from me!'

Her high-handed tone slipped into the background as my attention was taken by Bluecoat. He never took his grey eyes off me and I continued to stare back, despite Abby's increasingly loud demands for my attention. He simply tilted his head to the side and continued to smirk. Then I noticed his arm slowly raise and the gun at the end of his hand point in my direction. Everything seemed to slow down as I watched it gradually raise and straighten. He was going to shoot and I had nowhere to hide.

'Abby, run!' I hissed, taking a threatening step forward.

'Run, what the hell are you talking about, why would I run?' she said, twirling around.

I took my gaze off him for just a second and glanced back at her. 'Run,' I calmly whispered, before turning my attention back to Bluecoat.

I'd been here before, hell this was my world. I knew that everything would be slower, that I would somehow step out of the universe and all its colours and become a passenger watching from the side-lines as the eternal fight between good and evil played out in front of me. A constant struggle for supremacy with no eventual winner, it would seem. Sounds became dull and distant, movement slow and languid. Smiles crept slowly across faces and hair rolled gently over shoulders. The air smelt of anticipation, mingled with a large dose of wood polish. I couldn't hear her anymore but I knew Abby was continuing to prattle on. My breath was drawn out in one long cavernous sigh. My leaden legs felt like dead weights and my hands tingled pleasantly with anticipation at what lie ahead.

The first true sound was a gentle 'poof' as a bullet chewed into the upholstery of an antique chair to my left. The second was of an old lady to my right as she drew in her breath and screamed at the top of her lungs. At first everyone just stood looking glassy eyed, wondering if the old dear was mad. Some even smiled sympathetically. Then they spotted him standing there, his arm raised, the gun gently smoking from its elongated barrel. That was when the spell broke, that was when all hell broke loose

'No, no, what the hell?' Abby was still stood there, looking in his direction, gently shaking her head from side to side, not willing to believe the scene in front of her.

He sent one more sloping smile in our direction then turned on his heels and disappeared.

'Come on!' Without thinking I grabbed Abby's arm and began pulling her forward.

'What are you doing?' She pulled her arm away violently and stared at me with questioning eyes. But I wasn't in a mood for questions right now, he was getting away.

'Come on, Abby!' I grabbed her a second time and pulled her with me. This time, she followed without protest.

I rushed towards the spot where he'd been standing only seconds before, trying desperately to avoid terrified tourists as I went. My dad would no doubt have told me this area was the cross hall landing that led to the rest of the complex. I reached the spot just in time to see his trailing coat disappear behind an archway that led out of the hall proper. Abby reached me a second later and immediately grabbed my shoulders and spun me around to face her.

'What's going on? That was gun fire, why is he shooting at you, Danny?'

I shook my head at her and turned to run after him, no longer caring if my demanding ex-girlfriend was following or not.

The world suddenly became a blur of oak cabinets, leather bound books and whitewashed walls as I rushed through a maze of rooms.

'That's the Faire Chamber, Danny, look at those wonderful putti figures on the fireplace.'

'Not now, Dad.'

I continued to see glimpses of blue as I sped from room to corridor to room, quickly becoming lost in the haze of history surrounding me. I could have been in the Armoury or the fourteenth century, I wasn't sure which. Some tourists and the odd attendant rush alongside, while the occasional group just stood and stared, no doubt wondering what all the commotion was about. People breezed across my path and I brushed them aside like reeds, intent on following the flashes of blue. The air was greasy with panic and fear, it hung like a fog, chilling you to the bone. The sound of voices was thin and reedy, the noise more urgent than normal, more desperate to get out. Abby squeaked loudly next to me, imploring me to stop and explain.

I ignored her breathless questioning, she'd just have to follow or get lost in the fog. After a while, the bodies thinned out and we entered a quieter part of the complex. All that remained of the bedlam we'd left behind was the odd murmur from Abby, that and the constant thought of him.

We went through yet another heavy oak door and dived out into the bright light and heavy air of a languid summer afternoon. The light blinded me for an instant, speeding colours to monochrome as I scanned around trying to get my bearings. We were in the inner ward but had come out of the castle from another exit. The angles threw me until I saw the familiar grassy area in front of the main entrance and the gas van still parked half on and half off the verge. The madness from inside didn't seem to have reached here yet but it wouldn't be long before it did.

'I saw him, I saw him come out this way,' I hissed, half to myself.

'Oh my God, Danny, what have you done? Why are you following him? What the hell has he done?'

I turned to her, momentarily taken aback by her barrage of questions. 'What the hell has he done?' I spat at her. 'What do you think?'

She looked at me with realisation dawning on her face,

her eyes betraying the inner struggle as she tried to come to terms with the possibility hidden in my question.

'Yeah that's right, he killed my dad.'

'But that can't be.' she said, and trembled.

'Oh can't it, and why's that then, Abby? Because bad things don't happen to nice people? Or maybe because in your world things like that only happen on TV?'

'Oh, my God, please tell me it's not true.'

'Oh it's true, my dad's dead and your precious brother killed him!'

'Clive?' was all she could ask in a timid whisper.

'Yeah, the not so wonderful Clive, a true black sheep now, then, eh?' I looked away from her in disgust and scanned the inner ward for any signs of her brother. I couldn't bear to look at her in that moment. She was a real link to everything that was wrong. She was his sister, his family, a connection to the prey. But she was also an innocent bystander, a potential casualty of the war and I didn't want to include her in that equation if I could help it.

'Danny.' I felt a gentle tug on my sleeve and looked around to see tears falling down her pretty face. 'Babe, I don't understand. He wouldn't do something like that.'

'Well, I was there and I can tell you that he could and he did.'

'The news just said that your dad had been shot, they didn't say anything about the shooter,' she stuttered.

'That's because they don't know who it is, but I do, Abby, I do, babe! That's why I'm here, that's why I'm chasing him, that and because it's great exercise of course.'

She stepped away from me, her eyes downcast, and droplets falling from her face and onto the gravel below. Shaking her head she mumbled her disbelief as she continued to back away.

I left her in turmoil and continued to search the area for her murderous brother. I'd have to deal with her later; right now I had bigger fish to fry.

One or two tourists began to stumble out onto the inner ward from the castle complex, blinking in the sun and floating around in a daze just as I'd done moments before. A mum came out holding her trembling daughter close to her chest. An old couple helped each other to a bench close by, the guy clearly relieved to be out but still wary and confused. More people followed, their heads lolling from side to side expecting to see the shooter at any moment.

I knew that things would soon get too busy for me to spot him easily and I was getting more and more concerned that he'd got away from me once again when I spotted him at the other side of the ward. He slid out from behind a sleek black jeep and began fumbling with the door to the driver's side.

'Clive!' I yelled at the top of my lungs.

The scream pierced the semi quiet of the dazed and confused chatting surrounding us. He spun on his heel and our eyes locked once again, only this time he looked startled rather than smug.

'Clive?' I heard Abby ask as she joined me. Pleading with her brother in one simple word.

'That's him, that's the man with the gun', the old guy shouted to the rest of the group, creaking out of his chair and moving towards Clive. A rising siren of concern slipped through the throng of lost tourists as they spotted the gunman once again.

Seeing the challenges begin to mount up in front of him Clive did what was expected and raised his gun, almost daring us to take him on.

Panic returned as people pushed each other to get away from the madman with the gun. The little girl began to cry and the old guy's wife took him firmly by the hand and pulled him away.

Clive began walking towards us, his arm held out straight once more. Abby moved forward, her arms reaching out, pleading with him to stop and put the weapon down. For once, I didn't know what to do. Abby had brought a new dimension to the contest whether I liked it or not. Whatever I thought of the monster in sky blue, he was still her brother. She loved him, faults and all, and like any concerned sister I was guessing she just wanted to help and to understand. Perhaps she could make him see sense when all I could do was hope to catch him. Perhaps love of family trumped revenge after all. Maybe he would stop for her, run towards her like some lost puppy, fall into her arms and cry like a baby. Yeah and maybe Berwick Rangers would win the European Cup!

Clive's arm began to waver as his sister continued to plead with him from a distance. With her back to me and the noise of the tourists scrambling for cover rattling in my ears I couldn't hear what she was saying but I could see the pain in his eyes and the doubt scampering across his face.

She turned towards me halfway through her next sentence and quickly smiled that heavenly smile that said 'I've got this, Danny, I'm in control. Don't worry, everything's going to be okay. We can go for pizza and ice cream later, what do you say?' That was when the wind hit me.

12 - Oswald's escape

First of all there was a flash of pure white light, followed by an angry fire of orange and black. The wind struck a millisecond later, a powerful gust that lifted me off my feet and hurled me backwards and down. An almighty wall of sound accompanied the wind, slicing through my brain and rattling my rib cage. I was aware of the ground coming up to meet me and bits of stuff hurtling past my ears and nose. The wind continued to rush over me. It dragged at my clothes and pulled at my shoes. I lay there with my body screaming at me once again. Strangely enough I was use to this now and lay there until the wind and the pain subsided. I knew, instinctively that I was okay. I'd hit the ground on my back and I'd have a hell of a bruise but that was about it.

As the wall of sound echoed away, I opened my eyes and looked up into a turgid blue sky crawling with inky black smoke. Lifting my head I looked around, expecting to see a scene of devastation but seeing manicured lawns and radiant coloured flower beds instead. I'd been spun around somehow during the explosion. Even so the screams and moans from the confused and frightened tourists still surrounded me.

I saw Abby lying not too far away. She was leaning on her side and coughing hard into the ground. I rolled over onto my stomach then pushed myself up onto my knees. I didn't trust myself to walk just yet but I had to get to her and make sure she was okay. Crawling slowly like a toddler find-ing his way in a strange new world, I wobbled over to her and reached out gently to touch her shoulder. She turned her blackened, tear-streaked face towards me. It contained one simple question.

'I don't know,' I croaked.

Over in the corner of the ward, the remains of the gas truck stood mangled and blazing. He'd done this. That was the only explanation, it had to be him.

'The truck, explosion, Clive,' I rattled through dry coughs and splutters.

'What do you mean?' Abby croaked back.

I scanned the rest of the ward and saw a glimpse of a black jeep disappearing around the corner of the inner wall, heading out and away.

'Abby, we have to go.'

'I need a doctor, I think my ears are broken,' she replied.

'No, we have to go. Your ears will feel better soon, it's just the noise from the explosion. Mine felt like that too and they feel better already. Come on, we have to go.' I was lying of course, my ears were ringing just like everyone else's, but I couldn't let that stop me, he was getting away.

I staggered to my feet and tried, as gently as possible to haul Abby to hers. She protested and mumbled something about waiting for the police and an ambulance, but I couldn't let them stop me, anyway things were different now. In the instance of an explosion, Abby had become a casualty of the chase, even if she didn't know it yet. I couldn't let her help them. I couldn't let her tell them what she knew. She was my new best friend and I had to keep her close.

With a gently insistent push, I steered her away from the carnage and over to the other side of the plush green lawn. Tourists and staff alike stood in dazed and confused groups, some crying, others staring off into space. The mum was still consoling her child but the old dears were nowhere to be seen. Perhaps the fireball had consumed them on its way to heaven and they were now sitting at the right hand of God, just like my dad. As we reached the end of the ward and began walking down the hill, past the mock throne, I saw men rushing up from the gatehouse, there was clearly no way out there.

'Okay, follow me, we have to get out of here as fast as we can.'

Abby looked at me blankly for a moment, as if she didn't know who I was. Then she shook her head to clear it. 'What do you mean? We have to get to the police. My brother just blew up a truck for God's sake!' Her sentence finished with a slight hysterical quiver; she was just about keeping it together.

'No, you don't understand', I replied in a gentle voice. 'We have to get away. If we go to the police now, your brother will be in all kinds of trouble and so will I.'

'What do you mean, how much more trouble can he get into? Why on earth would you be in trouble?'

'I left the scene of a crime, Abby, I'm pretty sure that's a crime. Besides, we can help Clive if we get to him first,' I lied. 'I don't want him to end up in prison. He didn't set out to hurt my dad but something made him do it. I have to find out what that is and help him if I can. If we go to the police now we'll never know and we won't be able to help him, don't you see?' I moved in closer to her, shielding her from the chaos behind us, willing her to see me and only me. Hoping she heard me, needing her to listen. 'Abby, will you help Clive?'

She looked at me with flat grey eyes, her expression as stiff as a statue, her hair playing across her forehead the only sign of life. 'Okay, but we have to involve the authorities as soon as we get him. We'd be in even more trouble if we didn't do that.'

'Okay, I promise, one word and he's theirs. Come on, we have to go.' I grabbed her arm, less gently this time and began marching her over to the far end of the compound.

'Where are we going, the exit's the other way?'

'Flour and windmills,' I replied.

'What? You've gone daft. What are you talking about?'

'I know another way, a quicker way. One with no police or guards.' Actually I didn't until that moment. It was crazy and she'd never go for it, but I'd got her this far so I figured it was worth a shot.

'Another way? It's a bloody castle, Danny; they didn't make loads of lovely doors just for us to use. If you're thinking of the battery gate, it's been locked for ages.' Trust Abby to know everything about the place, just like her dad.

'No I wasn't thinking about there, come on I'll show you.'

We passed a few curious tourists making their way over to where all the commotion was, but they weren't interested in us so before I knew it we were at the far edge of the castle looking out over the gently sleeping countryside.

'You remember this old windmill?' I said, pointing to the smooth round turret to our right.

'Yeah it's been a flour store too, what about it? We can't go that way, it doesn't go down to the village, it's just a store.'

'No, I wasn't thinking about that, I was thinking about St Oswald.'

'You have got to be kidding me. St Oswald's gate? Danny that's madness.'

This part of the castle was known as St Oswald's gate, not because there was ever an actual gate here but because the saint got out of the castle by climbing over the ramparts next to the windmill and using a crumbling buttress to climb down and escape the mob who wanted to chop his head off.

'It's the only way, and we can do it if we're careful.'

'No, you're mad. I'm going to get the warden.' With that she turned away from me, her hair whipping across my forehead as she moved past. I reached out and grabbed her arm once more.

'Abby, wait. We can't go back. The whole place will be locked down by now and Clive could be anywhere. If we don't go now we'll never be able to help him or my dad don't you see?'

'If we try what you're suggesting we won't be able to help him anyway, because we'll be dead.'

'No, we can do it. It's not as hard as you think and I know a way we can do it safely.'

She stared at me with disbelieving eyes and began shaking her head vigorously. 'Safely. Dan, you want us to climb over the wall and try to get to the bottom, which is about a hundred feet by the way, without breaking our necks, there's no way we can do it safely.'

'We can, let me show you, and if you're not convinced, then we'll just give ourselves up to the police. Okay?'

She stared hard at me again. I could feel the uncertainty flowing out of her in waves, but I also knew she wanted to help her brother and that meant keeping him away from the police. Abby was a bit of a thrill freak like me. I guess it was all those days cooped up in the castle surrounded by stuff that was a thousand years old. After a while you just wanted to get out, let your hair down, feel the grass beneath your feet, that kind of thing. My dad must have felt it too, that's why he loved bouldering so much. I'm ashamed to admit it but I knew this was one of Abby's many flaws and I was counting on the fact that she wouldn't be able to resist the idea once the shock wore off and the thrill of it started to seep into her bones.

'What if we fall?' she asked quietly. There was anticipation in her voice now, I could hear it at the edge of her question.

'We won't. Like I said, I've got an idea that will make it easier.'

She looked away, out over the wall and into the abyss below, then turned her head slowly and stared at me once again. 'Okay, but no promises. If I'm not convinced, we go and find the cops and tell them everything we know.'

I just about managed to keep the grin off my face. 'Sure, whatever you say, but I know it'll be okay.'

I walked away from the wall and over to the dig my dad had been so proud of. 'Help me get one of those sheets of hardboard,' I said as I climbed over the rope and knelt down at the side of the dig. I began explaining my idea before she could ask. 'These boards are quite sturdy, they have to be in case one of the tourists is a nutter and decides to climb all over the pits. But they're also quite easy to move. I figure we can use one as a bit of a bridge between the sections of the old wall that fall away from here and down to the ground below. We climb across it then pull it with us. There are only three sections and then we're quite close to the ground. We can jump the rest of the way and there's loads of ivy down there so it'll be like jumping onto a soft mattress.'

'You've thought of everything,' she replied as we grabbed the ends of the board and began hauling it over to the wall.

Once there, we rested the board on the top and took a bit of a breather. Abby slid to the ground, resting her back on the cool grey stone. 'At least my hearing's come back', she muttered, shaking her head gently from side to side. She sat there for a moment gazing into space then turned towards me. 'Why the hell would he do that, Dan?'

'I don't know, desperate I guess; he doesn't want to get caught.'

'I never thought my brother would ever get that desperate, even if he has done some stupid stuff in the past. Then again how desperate are we? Using some bloody old board to climb over a castle wall.'

'That's not desperate that's inspired,' I replied with a grin. In truth, I'd only just had the idea to use the boards. My first thought was to try and jump between the sections, but I knew that was just a bit too dangerous, even for Abby.

This side of the castle was much steeper than the wall I'd climbed up on the other side, due to the fact that the castle itself sat on top of a hill that ended in a sheer drop at this side. Our way out, St Oswald's Gate, was really a set of three separate, crumbling sections of a wall that ran away from the main wall at right angles. They sloped down and away from us until the end of the last one was just a couple of metres or so above the ground. Each section was separated from the other by nothing but clean air and I was hoping the board was long enough to reach in between and give us a sturdy bridge to cross over. From where I was standing it looked like a set of giant's teeth, old and pitted and covered in a patchwork of lichens, moss and bird poo; probably from that damn gull.

'Okay, let's see if it'll reach, then you can decide if you want to give it a try.'

Abby stood up with a groan and grabbed hold of one

end of the board. Together we slid it across the open space between the wall and the first tooth. It scraped along, sending gravel and stones hurtling down into the gaping maw of emptiness below. Just when I thought it wasn't going to reach, it slapped down onto the end of the first section of wall with a satisfying whack.

I took a deep breath and turned an expectant look at Abby. 'Well, what do you think?'

'Give it a bit of a shake.'

I slapped the board hard a couple of times and gave it a thump with my fist. 'Solid.'

'Until you get on it then it snaps in half and you hurtle to a horrible death.'

'Well, let's see,' I replied, climbing onto the battlement.

'Careful, Dan,' Abby whispered through clenched teeth.

I took one quick look around the outer ward to make sure no prying eyes were watching us, but it was as deserted as when we got there. A gentle plume of black smoke rising into the heavens away at the other side of the castle was the only movement I could see. Taking a deep breath I rose to my full height and with arms outstretched stepped onto the board. I knew I couldn't hesitate or show fear at this crucial moment or Abby would call me back. Better to face a horrible death than that. I felt the board gently start to bow as I put my weight onto my front foot. I knew I had to step across as quickly as I could but that was also the biggest risk. If the board gave way I'd have no chance.

'Be careful, Dan,' I heard my dad say inside my head. 'Just turn around and go back, nothing's worth this kind of risk son.'

'It's worth every risk, Dad.'

'Did you say something?'

'No just psyching myself up that's all.' With that, I stepped forward and put my faith in the thin strip of wood beneath my feet. The board began to bow more steeply as it took my full weight and for a second I was convinced it was going to snap and send me tumbling down, but it steadied and I moved forward as quickly as I dared. The hairs on the back of my neck stood up in a now familiar pattern and my stomach began to complain once more. The ends of the board ground against the brickwork in protest as I made my way forward and it felt like I was standing on the make-shift bridge for an age, then suddenly I felt hard stone beneath my feet and my stomach lurched in relief. Taking a deep breath, I steadied myself, then turned to face Abby. 'See, piece of cake.'

'Did it feel okay?'

'Yeah you saw, it held fine.'

She looked at me uncertainly then took one last look around before climbing onto the top of the wall with ease and placing her foot, tentatively, onto the board. I was sure she was going to be fine, she was lighter than me and it took my weight easily, but I crouched down and placed my palms on the board just in case and to give her a bit of reassurance. In truth, it wouldn't make a blind bit of difference if the board snapped. Slowly at first she stepped forward with her arms outstretched; the board bowed again just as it had with me but she walked across easily and fell into my arms with a sigh of relief. A heady mix of perfume and sweat filled my nostrils as she pressed against me, then she was gone, stepping away to survey our perch on the top of the mouldy tooth.

'OK now for the hard bit.'

'What!'

'We have to drag the board across and that won't be easy, so make sure you get a firm grip or it'll tumble down to the ground and we'll be up the creek so to speak.'

'You could have mentioned that before we started.'

'I did, remember? Either way we're here now so we might as well get on with it,' I replied. I crouched down and took a corner of the board firmly in both hands before she could respond to my comments. Grumbling under her breath, Abby crouched down at the other corner and took hold.

'Okay, get your fingers underneath first, then pull the thing until it's over onto our side.' I felt the rough edges of wood dig into my hands as I took hold and prayed I'd got this right. 'Okay, pull.'

The board moaned and creaked as it scrapped along the edge of the tooth, then suddenly dipped as the edge resting on the main wall fell away.

'Steady!' I growled as we took the board's full weight and began frantically pulling it towards us before momentum took it down. Together, huffing and puffing we managed to get the majority of the board over onto the top of the tooth before collapsing into exhausted heaps.

'That was not easy,' Abby gasped.

'Yeah but we know what to do now, so it'll be easier next time.'

'Oh yeah, next time.'

I lay on the rough uneven stone, conscious that she was lying inches from me. I could almost feel the heat radiate off her and knew that her scent would begin to touch me at any moment. I kept my eyes fixed to the heavens, concentrating once again on the single white cloud that refused to disappear. I figured if it filled my vision and my brain it would stop me doing something stupid like rolling over and kissing her. A silly thing to do at the best of times and insane while we were perched a hundred feet up a ledge during a crisis. She was still infuriating and delicious in equal measure, that had always been the case, whatever the circumstances, and I was finding it hard to stop myself.

'Are you okay?'

I jumped out of my reverie and shook my head to clear it. 'Yeah I was just wondering why that cloud's still there. I've been seeing it all day.'

'Honest, Dan you do say the silliest things. That isn't really important at the moment, is it?'

'Well, no, but sometimes you think the weirdest things at the strangest times. At least I have been today.'

'I'm really sorry about your dad.'

'Thanks. I'm sorry you have to go through this and that your brother did what he did, you didn't deserve that.'

'No, don't even think that. It's your dad that's suffered, and you. My brother will pay, I promise, and, well, I was just in the wrong place at the wrong time I guess.'

'Or the right one depending on your point of view.'

'What do you mean?'

'Well, it's good to have you here to help, even if here is a very dangerous place.'

'Don't mention it, babe.' She smiled that gorgeous lop-sided smile I hadn't seen in ages and my stomach did a flip for the millionth time that day, although this time it was more than welcome. I sighed loudly and stood up. 'We better get going, someone is bound to come over here eventually and we'll have a hell of a time explaining this if we're still here.'

I began dragging the board noisily down the slope of the tooth. It had a flat first section that had enabled us to lie down but it gave the impression that it wasn't as steep at it really was. I had to grab hold of the board and steer it carefully down the slope until we reached the bottom otherwise it would simply slide down and tumble away. The end of the first tooth was steeper and more decayed than it appeared from the top of the wall. It was difficult to get a proper foot hold and haul the board over the side at the same time. 'We're going to have to be careful here. Grab hold tight or the thing will go over the side.'

'I know what I'm doing, Danny; you just make sure you grab hold.'

We stood on either side of the board once more and lifted it into the air. There wasn't a nice flat wall to take its weight and guide it along this time. Brute strength was all we had and I was nearly on empty. I hissed through clenched teeth as the heavy board began to tremble in my hands. It inched out over the abyss and I realized with a start that we weren't going to make it. With nothing to rest it on it was the length of our arms that would determine how far the board would reach and the edge of the second tooth looked miles away. The tip of the board began to dip and then tremble as our strength started to fail.

'Throw it,' Abby huffed, 'throw it now!'

I gathered what strength I had left and lurched forward. The board raised slightly into the air then collapsed downwards. The tip clattered into the edge of the second tooth with a crack. It wobbled for a second then settled into place. I dropped my end of the board at my feet and let out a huge sigh of relief, before tumbled backwards onto my butt.

'That was close.'

'I don't think I've got enough strength to do that again. How the hell are we going to reach the last one?'

'It'll be okay; anyway, let's worry about that when we get across. We can rest a bit when we get over and then see how we go. It doesn't look as far from here.'

I stood up before Abby's gloom could set like cement.

'We'd better keep going. The quicker we're across the quicker we can finish.'

I stood on the edge of the board once more, but with even more trepidation than last time. The other side looked to just reach the edge of the buttress and I imagined it bowing and slipping off as I raced across. The drop still looked long and I was sure it would be even further if I punched through the crawling ivy wrapping itself around the base before tumbling to the earth beneath.

'Careful, Dan, it doesn't look as steady as last time,' my dad warned.

'Yeah, ya think!'

With no other option I stretched my arms out again and tried to steady my thumping heart. The wind returned to lick across my face, whispering in my ears.

'It's a big drop, Danny, and you're a very big stone. It'll be fun watching you tumble down. You escaped us last time but this time we'll follow you down.'

'Stop it!'

'Stop what? I didn't do anything,' Abby complained.

'Sorry, just psyching myself up again.'

'Well, can you do it quietly?'

'Sorry.'

With an embarrassed cough I stepped onto the board and felt the all too familiar bow. Watching the far edge carefully I took a large step out and saw the board rise away from the lip of the second tooth. Panic lurched through me at the sight and it took all I had to bring my left foot forward and move out. As quickly as I dared, I walked across. A surge of fear sizzled through me as I went and I reached my destination almost in a blind panic. I was half way down the steeply sloping second tooth before I realized I'd made it. Scrambling to a halt I turned to see Abby chuckling gently.

'What's so funny?'

'You are. You looked like a crazy chicken racing across a busy road, very smooth, babe.'

'Yeah, well, why don't you give it a try, little Ms Perfect?'

'Okay, I will,' and with that she calmly walked over the board, taking the last stride in a hop and gracefully bowing on her arrival. It was just like old times, always egging each other on, always trying to outdo each other; we were obviously the perfect couple.

'Well, mine was harder; you saw that it would hold when I got across.' I mumbled sullenly.

'Oh yeah, your desperate scramble gave me loads of confidence,' she replied laughing. 'Come on let's get the board across then we can rest a bit.'

We knew what to expect this time and gave the board a good tug at the start to build up momentum. The wooden bridge slid across easily this time and we carried it down to the next gap and hauled it across without incident, sitting down gratefully once it was secured. I sat there with growing confidence. We were two thirds of the way there and no drama so far. A couple of heart attacks but that was nothing. I looked up to see the lonely cloud still sat in its empty sky, the tricky wind that had played catch with me all day, didn't seem to be able to touch it high up in its solitary perch.

'Are you really going to hand him over to the police when you catch him?' she asked.

'Of course I am,' I replied more sternly than I intended.

'I want to make sure he gets what's coming to him and that's not revenge. My dad wouldn't have wanted that. He has to face the consequences of his actions.'

'He's got a gun. How are you going to make him face the consequences of his actions when he's got a gun and all you've got is righteous indignation?'

'I don't call my murdered dad righteous indignation!' I shouted more loudly than I intended.

'I know, I'm sorry,' she replied quickly. 'I just mean he's got a gun and you haven't. I can't see how you're going to stop him and I worry about you, Dan.'

'It's okay,' I replied softly. 'I just know I can. If you'd been through what I've been through today you'd know too. He hasn't got it in him. He had loads of chances to finish me off and he didn't take them. He just can't do it and I know that he won't be able to when push comes to shove.'

'He *has* got it in him, Dan, otherwise he wouldn't have killed your dad, don't you see?'

'Yeah, but I don't think he meant to. I think it was an accident. They fought and the gun went off. That's why he's running. He'll get away if I stop chasing him now. I know it's strange after what he's done but I can help him, I know I can.'

'I wouldn't,' she replied tersely. 'If he'd shot *my* dad, he'd be a dead man right now. As it is I'm going to kill him when I see him, for what he's done. Not before I understand why he's done it though. Come on, let's get going before someone sees us.' With that she got up and brushed herself down. The conversation was over as far as Abby was concerned.

'OK, let's get off this rock.'

'What?'

'Nothing, it's a quote from a film, I like,' I replied, ladies first?'

'No, thanks, you can keep your chivalry. I want to make sure the thing holds, so on you go,' she replied, laughing.

'Wow that's so modern of you. Your concern for my welfare is touching,' I chuckled. I didn't think this time, I just walked, my head straight, my eyes facing front. I saw a spot on the horizon and walked towards it. I felt the board warping once again but thought nothing of it, I was going to get across, I was going to be okay and that was that. The bowing became more pronounced the further out I went and again I thought nothing of it, it had done this each time. I was nearly across when the board snapped and Abby shrieked. I instinctively turned towards the sound and saw her blonde locks disappear into the green jungle below the tooth. Somehow I managed to catch the rough edge of the next buttress before the board fell away. My hands scrambled for purchase on the rough, mossy stone and I knew I wouldn't be able to hold on long. I had to get up and onto the final column before my body weight took me below. My arms began to scream almost immediately. I felt my strength drain away like water racing down a pluck hole. I didn't have the strength after all my exertions and I could feel my grip quickly failing.

'Well, well, what do we have here? It's Danny! We have you now, Dan. It's taken a while but you can't escape us now.' The wind tickled up my back, making me shiver despite the desperate situation I was in. 'Let go, we promise to catch you,' it cackled.

'Let go, Dan, it's not as far as it looks. Let go, you'll be fine. Just remember to relax your body, Dan, relax and fall feet first.'

'Dad?' I croaked, before finally letting go.

13 - A CLEAR BLUE SKY

'**D**o you know a clear blue sky creates the most shadows and dark places?' asked the first shadow.

'As a matter of fact, I did,' replied the second shadow.

They stood as dark outlines against an ancient stone wall at the far side of the castle's inner ward, still as statues, quietly observing the scene of carnage around them.

'I don't think we can sort this,' the second shadow observed.

'I think you might be right,' replied the first.

An old man, dazed, confused and smelling of smoke wobbled towards them.

'Then again there may be one or two things we can do.'

The first shadow wobbled down the castle wall and slid over the grass towards the old man.

'Oh my, did you see that maniac blow everything up?' shouted the first shadow as it neared the confused old dear.

'Eh?' he replied.

'Did you see it? Did you see that guy in the black coat blow up that truck? Why the hell would he do that? How are you by the way?' asked the first shadow.

'Err, yeah, I saw it, I saw what he did.' The old man staggered forward then leaned over and crouched down on the ground with a groan. The shadow followed him down, nestling into his side as it settled beside him.

'He looked menacing through that beard, did you see? Menacing and ready to do anything, I'm not surprised he acted so violently.'

'Yeah, I know what you mean. Did he have a beard?'

'Oh, yes, a bushy red one, didn't you see?'

'Now you mention it I did, it was horrible, it made him looked a real bad 'un.'

'Exactly,' replied the first shadow, patting the man's arm gently.

The second shadow had, by this time, reach an old lady sat silently on a bench, staring at a perfect row of pansies.

'Are you alright, dear?' the shadow asked.

At first she didn't appear to have heard him, but she looked up as the shadow settled over her body.

'What did you say?'

'Are you alright?' asked the shadow once again.

'Yes I'm fine. Have you seen my husband, he needs his pills?'

'I'll help you look for him in a moment. Did you see the guy in the green overalls with the gun?' asked the second shadow.

'Yes, I saw him point the gun and fire, then whoosh!' She spread her arms out around her in a weak imitation of an explosion before plopping them back down by her sides.'

'Did you see the scar on his cheek, all white and horrible? It made him look very frightening.' asked the second shadow.

'Oh, my, yes!' replied the women, coming to life. 'I saw it, it gave me the creeps.'

The first shadow had now reached a young mum holding her baby close to her chest. She was sat in the middle of the lush green lawn rocking gently back and forth while groups of tourists staggered in front of her, the odd one occasionally asking after the baby's wellbeing.

'That baby is ever so well behaved,' observed the first shadow.

The mum looked up and was temporarily blinded by the sun. Blinded until the shadow crossed over her face that is.

'Yes, she's always been really good,' the mum replied looking away and continuing to stare into the distance.

'Why on earth would that horrible man put your little one in such danger? Some people are nothing but monsters,' the first shadow said. The mum just nodded in reply. Her baby stirred gently, raising its arms and gurning weakly. The mum tutted softly, putting her black, grimy finger into the baby's mouth.

'She's hungry but I don't know where her baby bag is.'

'Well, I can help you look for it,' offered the first shadow.

'Yes, thank you,' replied the mum vacantly.

'It's okay, I think he's gone. I saw him speed away in a posh Jag. Funny that, a bloke in a neat black suit driving a Jag blowing up a gas truck.'

'Yeah, funny,' replied the mum, 'the bloody rich get all the fun.'

The shadows crept from person to person, tourist to tourist, returning eventually to their spot on the wall.

'We better go, I hear sirens and we really don't want to be here when Mr Policeman arrives,' said the first shadow.

'No we don't,' replied the second shadow.

'We've done all we can here, let's go for a nice cup of tea and a bun.'

'That sounds really nice, can I have a scone and jam?' asked the second shadow.

'Well, of course you can, we both will,' replied the first.

14 - THE BEAST

I was plunging through a world of green: fern, forest, shamrock and pine. Olive greens raced past in a blur, apple greens scratched my face, jungle greens enveloped my world.

'Bend your knees when you hit the ground, Dan, bend them or break them.' I hit the ground at an angle, instinctively bent my knees to absorb the impact and fell sideways against the sloping castle hill. I came to an abrupt stop, my head covered by my arms, leaves and grass settling around me. Amazingly I felt nothing. I was either lucky or dead and was praying for the first.

I listened to my heartbeat in a moment of silence, waiting for my pain receptors to start blaring. Nothing happened so I twisted my head and unfurled my legs. My muscles groaned in complaint but no sharp pains rushed to meet me.

I took a deep breath and tried to see through the gloom. I'd come to rest against the side of the hill, my fall stopped by the angle of the earth. I stood up and my head punched through the ivy's canopy. I looked up and realized the fall was no more than three of four metres.

'That can be enough to kill you, Dan.'

'Thanks, Dad, but shut up. Abby, are you okay?'

At first only the wind replied and then a quiet, embarrassed voice said, 'I'm fine, nothing's broken. Hang on I'll be out in a minute, where are you?'

I looked around and saw that a path was just the other

side of the last tooth.

'I'm on the path, do you need any help?'

'No, I'm fine. I'll be there in a moment.'

I clambered through the thick ivy and underbrush and stepped gratefully onto the path. Amazingly no one was around. I was guessing that everyone had rushed to the castle entrance to see what all the noise was about.

'Come on, Abby, we have to go.'

'Okay, I'm coming out, but don't laugh.'

'What?'

'I said, don't laugh.'

I had no idea what she was going on about. What was funny about falling off the side of a stone column?

'Okay,' I replied slowly, 'are you alright?'

'I said I was fine,' she replied, standing up. Her hair, normally so meticulously arranged was in a bit of a state and she was sporting a new leafy clasp.

'Is anyone about?' she asked conspiratorially.

'No, but there will be soon, so get out of there.'

'Okay,' she replied, reluctance written across her face. 'But you promised not to laugh remember?'

I did my best to keep a straight face as she walked out of the underbrush and nearly managed it until she turned around to try and release her foot from the ivy.

'Danny, you promised!'

'I'm not laughing I'm releasing tension.'

Her suit trousers had been ripped from crotch to ankle and her bright pink knickers were clearly visible when she turned around.

'What the hell just happened?' I asked.

'I put my foot on the board to give it a bit more support and fell over when it broke, sorry about that,' she replied sheepishly.

'Nah, don't worry, there was a good chance of it happening anyway, it wasn't your fault,' I replied dismissively. 'Are you OK though? It was a bit of a fall.'

'Yeah I'm fine. So you thought it was going to break anyway, did you?' she replied with raised eyebrows.

'It's a good job my car isn't too far away.'

'I'd forgotten you'd passed your test, good, I'm sick of walking.'

We walked around the side of the castle complex, the wide expanse of an empty cricket field to our right, the high, domineering walls rising above us on our left. Muted sounds of sirens drifted over them and I imagined police and security guards racing around, trying to work out what had happened. An ambulance raced past us, heading up the winding road to the castle entrance, sirens blaring and blue lights flashing.

'I hope everyone's okay?' Abby muttered guiltily.

'Clive did this, not you.'

'Yeah, I know, but I should have stopped him.'

'How could you have? You had no idea what he was doing, or what he's capable of.'

'He's my brother, I could have said something.'

'He blew up a truck while you were in front of it, I doubt anyone could have said anything that would have made a difference. Don't beat yourself up about it. Come on, I need to sit down and you need new trousers!'

'Yeah, very funny.'

We got to the car without seeing anyone and I gratefully sat down in the passenger's seat with a sigh.

'I've got a room at a local B&B; we can go there to clean up and work out what to do next.'

'Why have you got a room at a B&B? Why don't we just go to your house?'

'No, we can't go there. Someone's looking after my mum and I don't want her disturbed. I booked it to give myself a break for a few days, so we might as well use it now.

'Fair enough,' I replied with a shrug. 'There's no point driving and looking for him now, he could be anywhere. He's gone and I have no idea where. I'm not really sure what to do next.'

'That's okay; we can work it out.'

The car felt stuffy and tight after I'd been out in the open for so long. Abby's close proximity didn't help either. She was a mess, her trousers were ripped, her hair was sticking out at various angles and smudge marks raced across her cheeks but she was still lovely and I was worried about the effect she was having on me. Now wasn't the time to be distracted I reminded myself once again. I closed my eyes and tried to forget that she was inches away. The car rocked gently as we trundled along the country road and before I knew it, Abby was shaking my shoulder.

'Come on, Dan, we're here, let's get to the room and get sorted.'

The B&B was more like an American style motel; luckily, this meant we didn't need to pass a reception and got to the room without being noticed. The room was simple and functional. A single bed, desk, wardrobe and old TV were all that it was furnished with. Drab cream coloured curtains stretched halfway across a vision of hay fields and I shuddered briefly at the thought of the combine ripping through mountains of straw.

'I need to freshen up; you can use the shower after me.'

She breezed across my view, leaving a slight scent in her wake. I lay on the bed and closed my eyes, imagining her lying next to me, smiling the warm smile she often used when we were together. I felt the efforts of the day begin to take their toll again as I eased myself around the bed. I didn't intend to sleep, there was too much to consider and the thoughts of Abby were enjoyable and distracting, but my eyes became leaden and I was asleep in moments.

The beast roared and snarled, its golden mane shaking with the effort, its black eyes, flecked with gold, boring into me, its hot breath washing over my shivering body. It stalked around me as I stood there naked and terrified, frozen to the spot with fear. It sniffed the air and roared once again. It was getting ready to pounce, to leap onto me and swallow me whole. I raised my arms and pushed them towards it, pathetically trying to ward it away. I knew it wouldn't do any good but there was nothing else I could do. I couldn't run, I couldn't fight, I could only die. The beast hunkered down on its massive legs, raised its hind quarters and got ready to pounce. This was it, the chase was over, there would be no revenge, only pain, anguish and loss. The monster leaped forward, its front paws stretched out, wicked claws flexed, a roar bursting from its jaws. All I could see, all I knew was the roar, was the jaws, was the blood red eyes. It was upon me, pinning me, consuming me.

'Danny, wake up, you're having a dream.'

I awoke with a start, my body shivering, a scream on the edge of my lips. Abby stood over me, her wet, cold hair ticking my forehead, leaving a streak of water that pooled into my eye socket.

'I'm okay,' I replied groggily, sitting up with a groan.

'You were moaning and rolling about all over the bed. That must have been some nightmare.'

'It was strange. I don't know where the hell that came from.' I looked up into Abby's concerned face, framed by straight wet hair. 'You better go and get dry. I'm sorry; I didn't mean to worry you.'

'It's okay, you didn't,' she replied, brushing her hair behind her ears, revealing a flash of gold earrings as she stepped away.

'What are they?'

'What are what?'

'Those earrings I've never seen them before.'

'They were a present from my dad. He had them made before he died. They're replicas of the beast.' She blushed as she replied, quickly turning and heading for the bathroom.

'Damn, I'm sorry, Abby.'

'It's okay, you weren't to know,' she replied, disappearing into the bathroom and shutting the door.

'The Beast's a small gold coin they found in the castle, Danny. The only one of its kind in the whole world. It's supposed to represent some kind of animal. It's a piece of Celtic morphological artwork. Quite beautiful and priceless. No one knows which animal it's supposed to represent but I've always thought it was a lion, Danny. After all, the castle was the seat of kings and the lion is a kingly symbol.'

'I suppose so, Dad; that makes sense.'

Whatever it was, it certainly was beautiful and a loving thing for her dad to do, quite out of character as it happens. But what the hell, he was dead, and you shouldn't speak ill of the dead.

I stood up and walked towards the window. It was full dark now and all I could see was my untidy reflection staring back at me. I was a mess, there was no denying it, but I was still here. 'Even though I have no idea where he was. I'd left the scene of a crime, the cops were after me and I was holed up in a room with my ex, who also happens to be the sister of my father's murderer. All in all, a great day,' I muttered under my breath.

I moved towards the bed and lay down once again. There was no danger of me going back to sleep, but I needed to try and get my head straight. I had to decide what I was going to do now, what my next move was going to be. More importantly, what his would be. After the castle, I figured he'd have to try and get away as soon as he could. He'd need to dump the jeep, it was far too hot. Then he'd need to get as far away as possible. His best bet was the train, but he couldn't be sure the police didn't have some sort of description of him already. At the very least, they might be on the lookout for a single man travelling on his own. At least I was lucky in that respect, I had Abby and her car. They were probably looking for me by now too, and they would certainly have my description. They might even think I'd done it. CCTV was bound to show me running towards the alleyway. It would also show me running after him, which meant they might know who he is. At least I hoped so. Witness statements would give them a good idea of what had happened; he was screwed.

Then I realised I was in a room with a TV. I grabbed the remote from the side of the bed and switched it on. It didn't take me long to find a local news channel telling the story of the explosion at the castle. They were blaming it on unknown suspects according to the news anchor, and were not ruling out terrorism. After a series of gruesome shots of the mangled truck and shell-shocked tourists they moved onto the second big news story of the day my dad's murder. The reporter was outlining the basic facts. A man was found shot dead in an alley way. Police were searching for a suspect or suspects unknown. Nothing about me or Clive leaving the scene of the crime. A live report from the scene didn't really add anything and a few eye witnesses only really managed to say they saw nothing of interest. The news quickly moved onto something else and I was relieved to see that the stolen combine harvester wasn't mentioned. I switch off the TV and stared out of the window.

Abby came back into the room, while I was deep in thought, and sat down next to me. She looked fresh and clean and totally gorgeous. She smelt gorgeous too, if that was possible.

'What did the news say? I heard you'd switched it on.'

'Nothing. The explosion at the castle's the main story then they talked about a man being shot in the town by unknown suspects. Come to think of it they didn't even mentioned my dad's name. Just said the victim was an elderly male.'

'What now?' she asked with a gentle sigh.

'I'm not really sure. I was thinking about it while you were in the shower and I figure he'll just want to get away. Public transport's probably best and he'll want to get to London. So the nearest train station that'll take him there is my bet. Have you got a phone, maybe you could just phone him and ask him what he's planning?'

'I don't have his number. What makes you so sure he'll leave anyway? From what I can see, he kept you running around the countryside all day when he could have just slipped away. There must have been some reason for doing that. Why leave now that he's given you the slip?'

'I was chasing him remember, he didn't get a chance to get away.'

'Really? And there was no time when you lost him?'

I remembered the time I'd lost him in the trees, and then again after crashing the combine. In truth, he'd had loads of opportunities to give me the slip and he hadn't until the castle.

'So what are you saying?'

'I'm saying he needed you to follow him for some reason. He needed to keep you close.'

'To keep me from going to the police.'

'No, it can't be that, otherwise we'd still be chasing him, right?'

'So what, then?'

'Well, isn't it obvious? You have something he wants, or you know something he needs to know.'

'How can you say that?'

'You were with your dad when it happened. Perhaps he thinks you have something with you, something that he needs. Did you have any bags with you?'

'All gone. I left them behind, except for my rucksack and I left that on a bus, so it can't be that.'

'Perhaps, and he must have seen that at some stage. What was in them?'

'Nothing, just climbing stuff and sandwiches.'

'But your dad was going to meet someone. That must have been Clive, so what was it?'

'We didn't have anything, Abby, I'm telling you.'

'Which leaves something you know; did your dad tell you anything?'

'When?'

'I don't know, this weekend, last week, a month ago, just after he was shot, any time.'

I pursed my lips as the image of him lying in my arms flashed in front of me. I could see him lying there, deathly pale, with pleading in his eyes.

'Arm, Dan, right arm, Oswald's right arm.'

'He didn't tell me anything, at least nothing I can think of right now.'

'Maybe it'll come to you later.'

'Maybe, anyway, your theory's flawed. If Clive wanted to keep me close, he's doing a bad job of it; he nicked a jeep and drove away remember.'

'That's true, so not something you know which means he already has what he wants and he's moved on. So he knows it's not on you and he now knows how to find it.'

'So, where? Back to square one?'

'Not quite; where's your dad been hanging out recently, except on rock faces and in that castle?'

'Usual places, university, home, university, castle.'

'Anywhere else, anywhere new?'

'Not that I know of. He's always hung around the same old crusty places. I don't get it why do you ask? What's this got to do with Bluecoat?'

'Who?'

'I mean Clive, what's it got to do with Clive?'

'Based on what you've said, I think my scumbag brother is after something. Something your dad had that Clive thinks you know about. If you clearly don't have it on you, and he saw that while you were chasing him, then he's figured out where it might be and that's where he'll be heading.'

'Well there's Holy Island, he always loved it there.'

'There's only one new place, Dan, don't you remember the lovely cakes and coffee in the converted stables?'

'Paxton House!' I blurted, sitting bolt upright on the bed. 'That's the only new place he's been to in years. Not for the history either, he loves the bloody coffee!'

'Are you sure? We have to be sure, otherwise we could end up somewhere miles away from him.'

'I'm sure, but if not there then Holy Isle.'

My dad was a creature of habit, which is why the bouldering was so out of character. He had places he went to on holiday, and nowhere else. He had places he visited and he had places he had to visit, that was it. I remember him telling me about Paxton House and raving about cakes of all things. Something totally unlike him, which was why it stuck in my head, or rather why his ghost reminded me about it.

Abby sat up on the edge of the bed like a cat ready to pounce. 'You're sure? Paxton House?'

'I'm sure.'

'That's what he knows, Dan. There's something at Paxton House and that's where he'll be tomorrow. We've got him,' she purred.

15 - INTO BORDERS COUNTRY

'The house was built between 1758 and 1763 by John Adam. It was for a local sophisticate by the name of Patrick Home. It's the finest example of Neo-Palladian architecture in the whole of Scotland, Danny. Did you know Patrick's mother was murdered by the butler? There seems to be a theme here, Dan.'

'Yeah, yeah,' I muttered under my breath.

We were sitting in Abby's car, in the picturesque grounds of Paxton House, located just over the border between Scotland and England. The house itself, a grand silver monument to noble excess, sat to our left. It winked in and out of view through the steady drizzle that patterned across the car's window pane. The drive to the house had been uneventful; unfortunately, so had the night before. After a refreshing shower I'd spent it skulking away in the corner on the floor. At least we'd spent the night in the same room, something I'd never thought would happen. Unfortunately, the crick in my neck was my only pleasant memory. The terrifying dream of sharp claws and thunderous roars hadn't returned, unless you count Abby roaring at me to stop snoring. It still felt strange being with her after the way we broke up. I half expected her to start throwing accusations at me or tell me to leave. I guess the most painful of things can bring people together, whatever their previous circumstances.

She sat quietly next to me and stared across the car park, seeing through the rain. Perhaps trying to see her brother, perhaps trying to make sense of how her life had turned in the past twenty-four hours.

'Abby, why aren't you upset?'

'What?'

'I mean, why aren't you more upset?'

She looked at me with a puzzled expression. 'I don't know. I feel kind of hollow, like there's a big space were all my fear and pain should be. I want to scream out, to shout and kick, but I just can't, do you know what I mean?'

I nodded slowly, I knew exactly what she meant. I felt the same way too, I had done ever since my dad came stumbling towards me, blood pouring over his shaking hands. My stomach had a hole in the middle of it and my heart was a block of stone. The only thing that got my blood boiling was the sight of him. That bright blue coat sent me reeling, I had to get it, to possess it, to hold it in my grasp. Perhaps then my heart would start again and I'd feel whole. I hoped my feelings were there deep down and all walled up. The emptiness was a necessity, the main thing helping me breathe. Stopping everything boiling over, stopping me from losing focus, keeping me on the right path. I should have been in borders country literally and figuratively. The border between what was rational and what was irrational but I wasn't sure yet if there were any consequences. What if this was it? What if I could never go back? What if I now had the emotions of a statue? An emotional cripple never able to feel anything, not able to laugh, cry, scream or mourn. They'd all think there was someone wrong with me, a cold fish detached from the world. Was that a price worth paying, I wondered? I'd only know when I finally had him, but of course by then it might be too late.

'Besides, you're not exactly brimming with emotion yourself are you? How do you feel by the way? Physically I mean,' she asked.

'It's like you said, I can't, at least not yet. I feel okay, got sore bits on my sore bits but I'll live. Are you sure he's here? I can't imagine why he'd know about this place.'

'Of course not, it's a hunch, but the best one we have right now, unless you've got any better ideas?'

'Well, no,' I mumbled.

'Well then. Okay, it's stopped raining, why don't we scout around a little? He may have left the car somewhere and walked here. If your theory's right, then he'd want to get here as soon as the place opened to give himself as much time as possible to search for whatever it is he's searching for. Are you sure you don't remember anything, Dan? Hasn't seeing the place jogged your memory at all?' she asked eagerly.

'Nope. This is the first time I've been here. Dad certainly talked about the place but we never visited it together.'

'Okay, you take the outside and I'll go and look inside; that way, one of us is bound to see him if he's here.'

'And what if one of us does see him?'

She laughed gently to herself. 'I hadn't thought about that. I guess we just try and talk to him before he bolts.'

'Or brings out his gun.'

'He won't do that.'

'You sound sure.'

She hesitated for a split second. 'He's no need to, right? He had the gun because of you, to keep you far enough away. But he'll figure he's lost you now so why would he keep it?'

'Yeah, except he's still on the run, so he might keep it to defend himself, and he has no idea where I am, so again he might need it to defend himself.'

I could see the blood rising in her face. She didn't like to be challenged. She always knew best and everyone should just get into line.

'That's not how it'll be, trust me.'

'Well, either way let's be cautious. If we see him, we follow him,' I replied, ignoring her instructions.

'What for? I thought you wanted to catch him?' She asked with a frown.

'I do, but I also want to know what he's after now and why it's enough to kill for.'

She stared at me for a long time then nodded her

agreement. 'Okay, we follow him if we get the chance; let's go.'

We got out of the car and separated without a word. I headed towards the gardens as agreed, glancing back to see Abby's blonde head bob away into the building. I scanned the manicured grounds for any sign of the stolen Jeep, hoping to see it huddled amongst the nearly new Fords and camper vans, but it wasn't there. Abby's battered blue car on the other hand stuck out like a sore thumb sitting there all on its own on the far side if the car park. If he was looking out for us, it wouldn't be hard to see.

'I guess this tests your theory Abby; is he here and how desperate is he to find this mystery package?'

My feet crunched over coarse red gravel as I made my way around the building and into the garden. The sound echoed off the white walls in a rhythmic beat, conjuring images of soldiers marching to battle, a sight this wedding cake of a building probably never witnessed. The garden itself was more of a posh lawn, its trimmed borders a riot of colour.

'Beautiful borders in the border country, Dan.'

'That's not half bad, I think you're getting better at this, Dad.'

I walked along the manicured lawn as casually as I could, just another tourist enjoying nature. But fear settled in the pit of my stomach every time I glanced at the building's dark windows brooding out at me, his face settled into the middle of every one. I turned my head away, trying not to think of him, focusing instead on the picture perfect garden. It stretched the length of the main building and the smaller one sat next to it. As I got to the far side, I saw that the whole area was blocked off from the front of the house by a large white wall, a brilliant white door with a sparkling golden handle sitting in its centre. I half expected a little handwritten sign to be tied to it saying 'open me'. Chuckling at the thought, I turned away and noticed a tree shrouded entrance to another section of the grounds tucked away at the edge of the lawn. A path fell away into the gloom and a small sign stuck next to it proclaimed that it was the entrance to the Teddy Trail.

'Teddies and Alice, this is turning into a real wonderland.'

I reached the path and looking down the trail saw it snake downwards into emerald and ochre coloured trees. I had no idea where the path led but he could have used it to come up to the house without being seen. With nothing else to see, I turned and made my way back towards the house, avoiding eye contact with the sightless windows as I went.

I was met by a large, red faced women smiling behind a riot of curly, red hair as I walked through the opulent entrance to the building.

'The next tour will start in twenty minutes, dear.'

'Oh, I don't really want to go on a tour, I was just planning on taking a walk around myself.'

'I'm sorry, entrance to the house is only allowed on an authorized tour, dear, and the first one started half an hour ago. I'm afraid you'll have to wait until the next one; it'll start soon.'

'Okay, I'll go and wait outside.'

'We have a really nice cafe you can use if you like? Some people are already waiting in there. The cakes are to die for.'

'Oh, okay, where is it?' I swivelled around looking for the entrance and an opportunity to get away from her; apart from Abby, she was the first person I'd really spoken to since the old dear on the bus and I didn't want her remembering me.'

'Just follow the signs dear and be back here in twenty or you'll miss the next tour.' A printed sign was taped to the wall next to a long narrow corridor. It announced 'This way to The Stables cafe.'

'Okay, thanks.' I turned and headed down the corridor. I didn't have a penny to my name but figured Abby was probably in there already sat in a booth, seething at not being able to get into the house and no doubt convinced Clive was already taking the tour, checking every nook and cranny as he went. She'd probably already convinced herself his hands were clasped around his prize, congratulating himself on his brilliance. Abby hated to be bested at anything.

I reached the end of the corridor and stepped into a bright, warm room dominated by a large counter and a set of old horse stalls, converted into fancy booths, running along one wall. I saw Abby immediately, sitting as straight as a rod and as pale as snow in one of the horse stalls. My heart caught in my mouth when she turned to look at me, her eyes as wide as saucers, and the corners of her tight red mouth turning up at the edges. She clearly had a companion sitting opposite her, hidden from sight by the side of the stall.

I took a breath and turned towards the counter, trying to give myself a moment of calm, a lull before the storm.

'What would you like?' I turned towards the voice and met the slack gaze of the disinterested girl behind the counter.

'Coffee please, can you bring it over there? I'm going to join my friends.'

'It's not a waitress service you know.'

'Oh, I'm sorry, only, well...'

The girl looked at me and sighed. 'OK, just this once and only because you're cute,' she giggled, looking at me through hooded eyes and flashing her eyelids.

I turned away, smiling at her cheek and was met with Abby's cold gaze. Taking another deep breath I walked towards the stall.

At first I couldn't see anything other than Abby's frozen form. Then a hint of bright, blue revealed itself as the seat opposite her came into view.

16 - COFFEE, CONVERSATION AND CAKES

'Take a seat, Daniel; now we're all here we can order coffee, I hear the scones are to die for.'

He sat as still as a corpse, his gaze never leaving his sister. He wore the bright coat like a shroud hanging limply from his shoulders. His face was covered in day old stubble and his oily hair was matted to his scalp. The single eye I could see was bloodshot and his hands were folded carefully in his lap. I couldn't see the gun.

'Room for one more, Abby?' I moved over and sat down next to her as she shuffled along to give me room.

'This is cosy, all friends together, eh. Guess you just bumped into each other? What a happy coincidence. I bet that made you happy, Clive?'

He looked at me for a moment, carefully sizing me up. Running his tongue slowly over his cracked lips he breathed in slowly and asked me one simple question. 'Where is it?'

'Where's what?'

He snorted at me in response. 'You know what, Daniel.'

'No, I don't, Clive, so why don't you enlighten me before I rip your tongue out, you murdering bastard!' I was suddenly shaking with rage. How dare he sit there, alive and well while my dad was cold and dead? How dare he sit there and judge me with his eyes? How dare he sit there at all?

'Play nicely, boys.' It was the first thing Abby had said and it was spoken just above a whisper.

'You've got to be kidding me. This isn't a game, Abby. I'm sat opposite a murdering scumbag. The fact he's even breathing insults me. And now he expects me to have a conversation with him. I've got one thing to ask you before I reach across this table and pull your lungs out through your mouth, you monster. Why did you kill him, Clive?'

He looked uncertain in front of my rage, but he made no move to reply.

'Remember what we agreed, Dan,' Abby said.

'Oh, I remember, I just don't want to any more. Come on, Clive, answer the question.'

'I asked first.' I jerked forward but Abby was ready, she grabbed my arm and pulled me back into the seat.

'Is everything okay here?' It was the girl from the counter. She stood over us with my coffee in her hand, her gaze drifting suspiciously between us.

'Everything's fine, they're just glad to see each other.' Abby responded. 'Thanks for bringing that over, how much?'

'Three pound fifty thanks.' Abby scraped the money across the table towards her. The girl picked it up and turned away, but not before looking at me with questions in her eyes. Someone else who won't forget me.

I looked at him again then sighed; this would go nowhere if we just started attacking each other, even if that was satisfying. I did agree with Abby that we needed to find out what he was after first. It galled me to let him sit there, to let him breathe when he'd taken my dad away from me, but all that needed to wait. Finding out why was the first priority, retribution would come after. Anyway if I didn't like his answer, I could always break his legs afterwards.

'Three pound fifty for a coffee, the price of things today. What is it you want Clive? You're going to have to spell it out for me, and you better do it quickly because from where I'm standing, I see a murderer sat in front of me who killed my dad for no reason and I'm trying my best to stop myself from reaching over and screwing your head off.'

He looked at me with narrow eyes, a brief expression of confusion flashing across his face. 'Your dad didn't tell you?'

I let my rage settle behind my face before replying. 'He didn't tell me anything, I've no idea what you're after.'

'The Beast. He didn't tell you about the Beast?'

I looked across at Abby, but she was staring intently at the pale wooden table top, trying to avoid eye contact with either of us. One of her bright gold earrings winked behind strands of honey coloured hair as she brushed her fingers around her ear.

'The Beast? You mean that small gold coin they found during an excavation of the castle years ago? Why the hell would my dad be speaking to you about that?'

'Because he'd stolen it.'

'What?'

'Well, I say stole, he was more an accessory after the fact as the lawyers say.'

'You'd know all about that.'

'Quite. My wonderful daddy stole it, but your dad found out and let him keep it. Can you believe that? Two of the most upstanding pillars of the community are thieves, and they call me the black sheep of the family.'

'Why would my dad do that? Why would yours?'

'Who knows? Greed, arrogance, stupid academic reasons, I don't know. All I do know is my dad had it then he gave it to yours.'

'What about you, what's your interest in this?'

'That's simple, Dan; money. I owe a lot of it to some very bad people. If I don't pay them back, they'll take it from my legs and other parts of my anatomy, and that's if I'm lucky. The Beast is a great way of solving that little problem, it's worth millions and my pathetic daddy thought it was best kept in a drawer in his office, after he stole it, rather than give it to his one and only son to help him out of a hole. I guess he was going to spend the rest of his life poring over it and congratulating himself on how clever he was. The professor who tamed the Beast; it's a scandal really and he could never have hoped to get away with it.'

'So you killed him, didn't you?'

Abby shifted uneasily in her seat then looked up at me for the first time. 'He would never do that, Danny; how could you say it?'

'But he could kill my dad? Looks to me like he's got a taste for it.'

She looked over at him with haunted eyes. 'Tell him you didn't, Clive, tell him you would never do that.'

'I didn't kill my dad, or yours for that matter, Danny. Their deaths were accidents. Totally unavoidable if they'd done as I'd asked.'

'Clive!' Abby reached over the table and grabbed his arm. 'Oh my God, Clive, please tell me you didn't?'

'I already told you I didn't, Abby, calm down. Dad had a heart attack you know that. He pushed me and I pushed back. He fell onto the ground and began clutching his chest. I didn't know what the hell to do; I got the hell out of Dodge when I couldn't find the thing hidden in any of the draws in his office.'

'It was your fault, you caused it! Why the hell didn't you tell me?'

'And say what? Sorry about your dad, Abby, oh, and by the way, his heart attack was my fault!'

'He was your dad, too, Clive,' she whispered.

'Barely.'

She began to shake quietly in her corner, a single salty tear rolling down her perfect cheek.

'And what about my dad then, Clive? Was that just an accident too?'

'We argued, he pushed and I pushed back. He pushed again and I brought out a gun. He lunged at me, Danny. I didn't want to hurt him but he kept on coming. I warned him, I warned him I'd shoot but he didn't listen. He just didn't listen, so he got himself shot.' He had a faraway expression on his face. Pain flashed behind his eyes every now and again. His bottom lip quivered glossily, a small trickle of spit running from the corner of his mouth. 'I'm sorry. I didn't mean any of this, you have to believe me.'

Rage, uncertainty, pity, hatred. They all coursed through me while he spoke. I couldn't believe him. My dad wouldn't have been that stupid. He was the most prim and proper man I knew. Always giving back change if he'd been under charged, always helping mothers with their prams, and always giving up his seat on the bus to an old lady. The very idea that he'd help someone steal something and then get into a fight with an armed and dangerous man went against everything I knew about the man. But sitting there, looking at the hollow shell in front of me as it spoke, I suddenly knew he was telling the truth, or at least his version of it.

'If what you say is true, that my dad is a thief and you shot him by accident, why would he meet you in the first place? Why would he admit to it at all?'

'Simple, I've got a recording of my dad telling me all about it. I recorded him on my phone and sent it to your dad. It's very interesting, he admits taking it, then he tells me all about the remorse and guilt he feels. If only he felt so much emotion for his family. He told me he found out your dad was looking for it as part of some research project. Sebby boy had taken it quite legitimately for some research of his own. He could do that easily what with him being the castle's archaeologist, but he hadn't put it back, he'd replaced it with a fake one instead. One of the cheap replicas they sell in the castle shop, can you believe it? He knew your dad would notice straight away and then it was only a matter of time before he put two and two together and came up with my dad. So he got to him first and he admitted it right out. Said he was obsessed with the thing, said he couldn't give it up and asked his best friend in all the world to help him. Your dad agreed to keep quiet about it all, probably for old time's sake or something like that. That's what I had on him, Dan, that's why he was meeting me.'

'This is crap. My dad hated using a mobile phone, so how did he get the recording.'

'I emailed it to him; everyone has an email address, even him.'

My emotions continued to churn inside of me as I took

it all in. The truth is never easy, they say, and this was turning out to be the hardest truth of all. My dad was a thief. 'No matter what he'd done, you still killed him.'

He looked at me for a moment, weighing up his answer. 'Yes I did, there's no getting away from that. I'm truly sorry, he was a nice man; naive but nice. He didn't deserve that.'

I took a deep breath. 'So what now? I have no idea where it is, Abby has no idea where it is and you have no idea where it is. That's that I guess, time for jail.'

'Not so quick. You might not know where it is but our little conversation has confirmed my suspicions. I had to keep you close just in case you knew where it was hidden. Very clever of your dad to give me that impression but seeing as you don't and I've already had a good search of this old house, that only leaves one place left.'

'What do you mean?' I asked

'You know your dad was just like mine. He'd spend his whole life in one room if he could. I had a list of places I knew they'd gone to regularly. A very small list, two peas in a pod those two. I've eliminated the first couple and have one left. So if you don't mind, I'll leave you to your scones.'

I reached forward and grabbed his arm. 'Not so fast. Do you think I'd let you go that easily?'

He smiled at me, then gently prised my hand away from his arm. 'No I didn't. That's why I've brought along a friend.'

I snorted at him in derision. 'Do you think that'll scare me? Don't you remember the farm?'

'Oh, I remember it clearly. I also remember saying to myself, don't do it, Clive, you need him. He knows where the Beast is hidden. But you don't, do you, Dan? So there's nothing really stopping me now is there? As you said yourself, I've got a taste for it now.'

I looked into his face and knew he was telling the truth. There was nothing stopping him now and I'd fallen straight into his trap. He'd been waiting for us all along. He knew we'd either figure out he'd come here, or the other place he'd got on his list. It was a fifty/fifty chance and he'd guessed right. All he needed to do was find out what I knew or didn't know as it happens. I was now expendable.

'Of course, you don't know where it's hidden either, do you? You might know the building, but where exactly is it hidden? If I know my dad, he'll have hidden it well. You need to know him to work it out, Clive and I'm guessing you don't know him that well, so go ahead, shoot. Then run as fast as you can before the police catch you. Unless you're going to shoot Abby, the girl behind the counter and the old dears sipping tea two tables behind you of course. That'll give you a bit of a head start.'

He looked uncertain once again, this was getting easier. It was clear he was running on instinct with nothing more than a few ideas about where the Beast might be. It must have looked so simple at the beginning. Daddy would surely help him out, but he hadn't and things had gone south pretty quickly after that. He was facing problem after problem and getting more and more desperate by the hour. I was guessing he knew it too.

'The police are probably after you already, Clive. The town had CCTV. They saw you running out of that alley. I bet they've got mug shots plastered all over the TV and online. So go ahead, make it worse; you'll never get to the Beast before the police get to you.'

He sent a broad smile my way and shook his head slowly from side to side. 'You're a real piece of work, Danny, a true adversary. You're the only one who's kept me honest in a long time. Look after her for me, she's going to need your help when this is over.'

I turned to look at Abby still curled into the corner, one hand covering her eyes. When I turned back he'd already stood up.

'I'm leaving now and you're going to let me. I know you are, because I'm going to shoot my sister if you don't and you won't want that, will you, Danny?'

Abby turned with a start; looking at him with red rimmed eyes. 'What are you talking about, Clive?'

'He still cares for you, Abby, that's as clear as the pretty nose on your face. I'm sorry, I truly am, but this is bigger than the both of us. War always brings collateral damage, you know. Don't worry, though; Danny here's a sensible chap. He won't let things get out of hand, not like I do, isn't that right, Danny?'

I swallowed hard and let him casually walk away. He was right. No matter how much I wanted to chase after him and rip the gun from his hands I couldn't let him hurt Abby, or the other customers in the cafe. I let out a sigh, 'Now what?'

Abby didn't reply straight away, she continued to stare at the exit Clive had just used.

'We wait until he's away and then we go after him, what else do you think we should do?'

17 - THERE'S SOME-
THING ABOUT ABBY

He was already gone by the time we got out of the café. I scanned the car park for the stolen jeep but couldn't see it anywhere. So we did the only thing left to us, we got into Abby's car and set off in general pursuit.

'How far do you think he's gotten,' I asked anxiously.

'No idea, but there's only one road out of here.'

We raced down a small road, as fast as we dare. It twisted around and in on itself, forcing us into a stop/start chase.

'Abby slow down,' I hissed after a near miss with a large oak tree growing at the end of the road.

'I thought you wanted to catch him?'

'All we'll catch is the next big tree, if you go any faster, then its game over. Besides you don't want to attract attention.'

'OK,' she said with a sigh, easing her foot off the accelerator.

After a few more turns we came to a junction and stopped.

'Left or right?' she asked.

'Right. If we figured right that there are only two places left he could go that leaves Holy Isle.'

She nodded and turned right.

'If he's gone anywhere else we're done for.'

'I think you're right, Dan. You figured it was Paxton House or Holy Isle. You were right about the first, so there's a good chance you're right about the second.'

'OK, slow down and let's get there in one piece.'

'Right you are,' she replied, easing off the accelerator.

'How are you feeling?'

'I'm fine, what do you mean?'

'Your brother just threatened to shoot you.'

'I'm trying not to think about that.'

'Why?'

'Like you said we need to help him. The only way we can do that is by stopping him.'

'Fair enough, if it was me I'd be raging.'

'Oh I'm raging inside, believe me.'

Do you think he's telling the truth about getting into trouble and all that?' I didn't want to ask her outright if she believed him about her dad and the heart attack.

'I think so. He's been in trouble before and my dad bailed him out. I can't believe he would just leave my dad like that though. He might have been able to save him if he'd phoned an ambulance.'

'He's got a lot to answer for.'

'It's always been the same. I remember when we were kids, he was the one always getting into trouble. One time he stole an air gun from a shop and went around shooting at birds and dogs. He hit our neighbour's dog in the head and killed it. My mum was furious with him but Dad talked her around. They didn't even phone the police. He gave the gun back and Dad bought the neighbour a new puppy. I guess my dad has always been cleaning up Clive's mess. It must have been a shock when he refused to do it the last time.'

'Do you know what kind of trouble he's in?'

'Not a clue. But knowing Clive, it won't be something small. When he messes up he tends to go big. I bet he owes some major criminal a shed load of money and he'll get his legs broken if he doesn't pay him back. By the sounds of it he may already have left it too late to save his legs. It might even be too late to save his life.'

'I'm not going to all this trouble just to let someone else kill him. He needs to answer for his crimes.'

'You should have gone to the police in the first place, you know that right?'

'Yeah, but it's too late now. I'm an accessory after the fact. I don't mind though as long as Clive faces justice.'

'I'm really sorry about your dad. I didn't think Clive would ever do something like that.'

'Sounds like he got a taste for it when he left your dad to die. I'm sorry for your loss too.'

'We make some pair don't we?' she said with a thin smile.

'We always did.'

'He always had a dodgy heart. We just thought it had just given up on him. God! Clive was even a pall bearer. How could he do that after what he'd done? I can't believe he could be that cold, it was his dad. He was crying and I comforted him, what a bastard.'

'I don't understand how anyone could act like that. I'm sorry you got a brother like him.'

'While we're apologising, I'm sorry over the way I acted with you about my mum. I know you were only trying to help. I shouldn't have gone off the deep end like that.'

I was shocked at Abby's admission. She never apologised for anything she'd done in the past.

'Don't worry about it, you were under so much stress, it's understandable.'

'Ever since my dad died I felt like I had to hang on tight to everything. To control everything, does that make sense?'

'Kind of.'

'If I didn't control things, with my family I mean, I was convinced it would all fall apart. That I'd wake up one morning and my mum and brother would be dead and I'd be the cause, because I didn't do everything I could to keep them alive. I know that sounds daft but it's the way I felt. When I was able to sleep, which wasn't often, I would have this same weird dream. My mum lost in the sand dunes, you know the ones next to the castle?'

I nodded, I knew the ones she meant.

'She was lost in the dunes and I could hear her calling out to me and Clive, desperately asking us to help her. I would see Clive go after her, but I couldn't follow. Something was holding me back. I don't know what, but you know that feeling of total hopelessness you have sometimes in dreams? That's what I felt. I watched him disappear and I couldn't stop him. Then I heard him cry out and ask for my help. My mum shouted for help too. There I was, my body stuck in place, while I listened to my mum and brother cry out for help. I didn't see it but I knew they both died there. That's when I woke up screaming.'

'That's awful,' it sounded weak but it was the only think I could think of to say.

'Yeah, I guess I'm pretty messed up in the head.'

'We all have problems. Look at me, I'm chasing your brother across the countryside while my dad lies dead in some morgue. You think you've got mental problems.'

She smiled at that and nodded. 'Like I said, we make some pair. So what are we going to do if we do catch him, again?'

'My plan hasn't changed despite what he said in the café, I'm going to take the gun off him and I'm going to take him to the police.'

'But you could have done that earlier. He's going to threaten me with the gun no matter where we are.'

'But we'll be prepared for it next time and I'm hoping there won't be anyone about?'

'There will always be someone about, Dan. That's not going to happen.'

Abby was right. I should have stopped him in the café, but the presence of a few customers and the girl behind the counter had made me pause. How was it going to be any different once we got to Holy Isle? If anything there'll be more tourists.'

'We'll figure something out,' I replied weakly.

We spent the rest of the journey in silence. Both of us consumed by our own problems. Then as we rounded another bend Holy Isle rose dark and brooding out of the ocean like the hump of a giant monster breaking the surface of the sea. I'd been here many times before, the good professor loved the old church and the mead, not necessarily in that order.

I was guessing Clive thought my dad had hidden the Beast inside the little church sitting next to the ruins of a once great priory, or even in the museum next to it.

The Island had a long history. Famous for its ancient priory, founded by St Aidan and home to the holy man St Cuthbert. It was linked to the mainland by a causeway which flooded at every high tide. There was supposed to be a pilgrim's way across the bay too, but hardly anyone ever used that for fear of drowning. I used to love the stories Dad told me, when I was a child, particularly the ones about Viking invaders raiding the island and killing all the monks in the priory. I would imagine all the blood and gore covering the floor of the church. The mighty Viking soldiers, swords dripping with blood, smashing all the holy relics and stealing the gold, I didn't tell Dad about that of course, he wouldn't have approved.

We dropped down onto the causeway and made our way slowly across it. I looked ahead, hoping to see Clive racing forward in the stolen jeep but the road was empty.

'Looks like he's had quite a head start.'

'If he's here at all,' Abby replied.

We crossed the causeway and followed the road around the edge of the island until we came to a large car park. It was full of camper vans and family saloon cars and we spent an anxious few minutes driving round until we found a spot to park.

'I didn't see the jeep, did you?' I asked.

'No, but the place is full to bursting so we probably missed it. Where do we go from here?

'I think the museum is our best bet. It has loads of displays and Dad may have been able to hide it in one of those. That's what I figure Clive might think anyway.'

'It's as good a place to check as any,' she replied.

It was a relief to walk along a straight, flat road for a change instead of over ploughed fields or through dark woods, accompanied by the constant adrenaline rush pounding in my ears and bullets flying past my shoulders. The hole in my stomach was still nice and small too. I still wasn't sure if this was because we were still chasing him, despite our slow pace, or because I felt differently about the whole thing; either way, I was going to try and enjoy it while I could.

'Do you think the Beast is here, Dan?'

Her question took me a little by surprise. I thought she'd be focused on finding her brother, not some stolen coin.

'Why do you ask?' I replied.

'Well, if it's not here, then that's our next move, isn't it?'

'Yeah, maybe, but let's just concentrate on getting to the museum and seeing if it's here, okay?'

'Why? Don't you want to answer my question or something?' She said the last with a cute pout.

'Of course not. I just don't want to think about that right now.'

She looked at me for a moment with calm, calculating eyes, the pout melting slightly from her face, then she turned away with a sigh. 'Fair enough let's focus on looking here and catching him then.'

We continued down the road until we reached the edge of what constituted civilisation on the island – a pub/hotel, a couple of shops, and the odd ancient row of terraces, all huddled together and turned inwards against the normally biting wind and ferocious North Sea. On the glorious summer's day we were walking through they reminded me of sad lonely old men with their backs turned against the warmth. Strange in their stark contrast to the vaulted blue sky arching overhead.

The ruined priory sat away from the centre of the village on a small outcrop of rock, looking out over the wide expanse of the bay. A small church nestled against it on one side while the museum sat on the other, the odd tourist disappearing into the building, and reappearing moments later. There clearly wasn't much inside to hold their attention. We on the other hand were a different matter, we had loads to keep us entertained inside. I approached the entrance to the museum with a slight tingle of fear and anticipation. He might be inside that very moment, searching between the displays and trying to get inside glass cabinets without anyone noticing, desperate to finally get his prize.

A small sign in front of the entrance welcomed us to the 'Lindisfarne Centre, home of the Lindisfarne Gospels and Vikings on Lindisfarne exhibition'.

'The centre's also got a lovely garden and a really nice café, Dan.'

'Hello, Dad welcome back,' I replied. To be honest I'd missed him, even if he was another example of my growing madness. We went through the low door under the sign and entered a dim quiet foyer, full of displays depicting the priory through the ages. Just like the castle, I didn't expect him to be at the entrance waiting for me, but even so, a nervous spasm ran through me until my eyes adjusted to the gloom.

'What now?' I asked Abby.

'Are there any displays here about the castle and the Beast?' she asked in reply.

'No, there's some gold and stuff in the Viking display, I think, but the place is mainly about the priory and the gospels. Pretty boring really, I think that's why my dad liked it.'

'The Lindisfarne gospels are a real treasure of Christianity, Daniel. The originals are never allowed to leave the British Library but they very kindly donated a facsimile edition to the museum.' I groaned inwardly and hoped Abby hadn't noticed that I was talking to the air again.

'I don't think we should split up, Dan. I don't want to meet him on my own.' Her admission, while surprising, was understandable. It isn't every day that you chase after someone who'd threatened to kill you, unless you're me of course.

'No problem, the place is far too small anyway. If he's here, we'll find him quickly.'

'Okay,' she replied with a sigh, nervously scanning around the gloomy exhibitions. 'Let's just take a look around like proper tourists.'

'That shouldn't take long,' I replied with a chuckle.

We began walking through the island's past. It was full of screaming Vikings, Celtic crosses and the odd ancient farming implement. I was glad we didn't see a combine harvester in any of the displays; that would really have sent me over the edge. All too soon, we came to the last display room and found nothing but pictures of seals, razorbills and puffins.

'Those are called Tommy Noddies, Dan.' I ignored my dad's latest nonsense and concentrated on the Abby's anxious face.

'He's not here,' she said quickly.

'No, he's not here yet. Remember, he knew we were chasing him. He's probably holding up somewhere eating an ice cream and checking to see if I come out of here with the Beast. Or maybe he checked the priory and the church first? We're probably ahead of him, for a change.'

'So, what do we do?' she asked, biting her bottom lip in that appealing way she knew always got my attention.

'Simple; we wait. He can't stay away forever, and besides, I need a seat.'

'Let's go to the cafe, I'll buy you another coffee, you never got to finish that one earlier.'

'No, let's not. I've lost the taste. There's a small room over there showing really boring films about the island, let's wait in there.' I couldn't face another coffee shop incident and the video room looked nice and quiet.

We entered the 'Education Suite' as the video room was grandly titled, to the sound of fishermen dragging their catch up onto the beach. The narrator calmly explained in the smartest Queen's English, that fishermen had been fishing off the island for over a thousand years. The room consisted of cushioned benches facing a large screen inset into a padded wall. The only light came from the flickering screen. To my relief, the room was empty; I suspected that was the case most of the time, what with the rubbish they were showing. The odd horror movie would surely have brought in more punters I thought, as I took a pew as far away from the entrance as possible.

We sat there for a while in the semi darkness, each lost in our thoughts. The video played in a loop over us and I quickly became used to its images of farmers and fishermen and the lilting music of a sea shanty, sung by a grizzled old sea dog. After a while, the images and music all blurred into one and I began to feel my eyes get heavy when Abby broke her silence.

'Do you think the police are looking for you, Dan?'

'I don't know, I guess so. I must have been caught on CCTV walking down the street after my dad. They must know who he is by now and will be looking for me anyway.' I turned my attention back to the film and watched yet another fisherman haul in his catch.

'I do so love fishermen, don't you, they're just soooo smelly.'

We both turned with a start

18 - Mr Chomp and Mr Chew

'And yet I simply hate fish, what a shame.'

'Can I help you?' I asked.

A slight man stood before us looking like something out of a silent film from the 1920s. He wore a sharp pin-striped suit, spats, and a kipper tie that looked garish even in the gloom. A black trilby hat with a bright white sash was cocked jauntily onto one side of his head. His tiny moustache looked like it had been waxed to within an inch of its life. All in all he would have set a comical look, if it hadn't been for his eyes. They were the eyes of a wolf and they looked hungry.

'Oh no I don't think so; you see, I've been helping you. Now please tell me your name.'

'What?' I replied, thoroughly confused.

'Your name, please, I like to know who I'm helping, especially when it's for free.'

'Helping, what do you mean? How have you been helping me?' I was convinced that the little man was totally off his rocker but I thought it best to humour him in the hope that he would go away.

'Oh, lots of ways, my manic little friend,' he replied. 'We've been following you and Clive since yesterday, it helps pass the time you see.'

Somehow I kept my face straight, but inside a chill ran to the marrow of my bones.

'How do you know Clive?'

'We'll come to that; your name please.'

'Dan, my name's Dan.'

'Pleased to finally meet you, Dan. I am Mr Chew and my associate here is Mr. Chomp.' I noticed the man mountain standing at the entrance for the first time. He tilted his head slowly in acknowledgement of Mr Chew's introduction and I was sure I heard his neck crack as he did so.

'I need no introduction to Ms. Abby, of course; I know all about her. We make it our business to know about family members. May I sit down?'

'Please do.' I responded, waving vacantly to the space beside me while I tried to compute all the things Mr Chew had just said.

'Mr Chomp won't sit, if you don't mind, its best after all. Better to keep him at arm's length and all that,' he said leaning towards me and whispering conspiratorially as he sat down. 'Well, now this *is* cosy, and such a quiet spot, don't you think, Abigail?'

'Yeah, it is,' she replied, clearly as confused and concerned about our new friends as I was.

'So, how do I know about our mutual friend Clive, you ask? Well, let me update you on a few things, Daniel; may I call you Daniel, it's much more appropriate than Dan, don't you think?'

'Yeah that's fine,' I replied.

'Clive owes our employer a lot of money, Daniel, so much money that he's got himself in quite the spot. Now, normally, we are employed to exact the money owed in as quick and painless a way as possible. Painless for our employer, you understand, not for the debtor, who on this occasion is Abigail's naughty brother. However, this particular situation has had some added complications we had not foreseen, so I'm afraid our normal methods of extraction have become temporarily redundant. We've been forced to the side lines somewhat by Clive's promises of wealth for everyone and then his rather silly rampage across the countryside; what on earth was that boy thinking? But being the understanding souls we are, Mr Chomp and I have done our best to facilitate Clive on his journey, hopefully to our mutual benefit, you understand. So we've been forced to help you on a number of occasions, too, Daniel, or nobody would have benefitted from the fabulous wealth of that tiny little coin. Are you following me so far, children?'

We both nodded like puppets on a string.

'Good. Before you ask, we know all about the coin. Clive's told us just how much it's worth. As for you? Well, you have been somewhat of a naughty boy, haven't you, Daniel? Stealing combine harvesters, going for joy rides and crashing the thing. Blowing up gas trucks, such a naughty boy. But don't worry, Mr Chomp and I have taken care of it, haven't we, Mr Chomp?' The man mountain tilted his head again and smiled.

'We were going along nicely too, although the farmer did prove somewhat difficult for a brief moment. Yes going along nicely, until yesterday, that is, there's only so much naughtiness we can sort out you see, isn't that right, Mr Chomp?' Once again, the mountain nodded in reply.

'I didn't blow up the gas truck, that was Clive,' I replied meekly.

'Yes, we know, but he wouldn't have done it if you hadn't chased him, now, Daniel, don't you see?'

'Yes.'

'And now we find ourselves in somewhat of a pickle once again, an experience we are not enjoying. We were supposed to meet Clive here and put everything to bed so to speak. Unfortunately he doesn't seem to be able to keep our appointment. That's such a shame, a real pity. We might not be able to offer another one you see, and the consequences of missing our meeting may be quite severe for Clive, and for his family too, I'll warrant. Do you see my meaning, Abigail?' he said the last just above a whisper, quiet, yet full of menace.

'I didn't have anything to do with Clive and his madness,' Abby replied.

'Oh, I'm afraid that's out of your hands now, Abigail, Clive's seen to that. If we can't get what we want from him, then we'll have to look elsewhere,' he replied with a broad grin spread across his face, exposing his perfect white teeth, glistening with saliva and anticipation.

'Abby's done nothing wrong, she's had nothing to do with this.'

'Yes I know, it's such a shame really. It's the ones we love who we hurt the most, isn't that right, Mr Chomp?' The mountain tilted forward once again. 'We have lots of family and friend we love an awful lot, Daniel, I'm sure you realize that?' I nodded quickly, unable to give a verbal reply, my throat tight. Mr Chew slid slowly forward on the bench, never taking his eyes off us as he moved forward.

'I like this museum,' he said quietly. 'I've always liked history, it fascinates me. All that where we've been and where we come from. It puts me in a very good mood, and when I'm in a good mood, I'm always inclined to be benevolent.' He slowly lifted his arm and stretched out his hand, revealing the switch blade resting within. He depressed a sliver button on the handle with his finger and the sharp blade popped out with a click. He lowered his hand until the tip of the blade came to rest on the top of the bench in front. Then, slowly, deliberately, he began to make a circle with the blade, a soft scratching noise coming from it as it made its way around.

'Tell me, children, do you think this museum would burn slowly or go up like a rocket, all fiery orange and red? I really don't know, you see, but I think it would be fun finding out don't you? What would you do, Daniel, if you were standing outside and Abigail was stuck inside? Would you try to get in and rescue her or would you just stand there and listen to her screams? Have you ever smelt burning flesh? It's quite lovely, it smells of fried chicken. I don't think you'd want to eat what was left in here once the fire has gone out though,' he chuckled.

'And what about you, Abigail, have you ever burnt your finger in the fire? It really hurts doesn't it? Well what do you think it would feel like to have your whole body burn? Can you imagine the agony? I've tried to but it simply escapes me. How could anyone endure that kind of agony for long? I'm sure it would send you quite mad before the end.' He continued to make a circle on the bench in front of his as he spoke, his eyes now following the blade.

'I'm sure you believe me, children, when I say I'm deadly serious. It would be the effort of but a few moments and it's not like we're strangers to the odd fire, Mr Chomp and I. However, as I said, I'm in a good mood, and so is my employer it would seem. Quite unusual that, especially considering how many times Clive has let us down.' He took the blade off the bench and leaned backwards with a sigh.

'One last chance, and this time it really is the last Clive will ever get. I'll be returning to this lovely Island tomorrow at the same time. I just can't get enough of the scenery, all those marvellous birds. It really does put Mr Chomp in a good mood too, which is lucky for you. If he's here tomorrow, with the coin of course, then all will be forgiven. If he's not? Well let's not dwell on that now shall we?' He got up and started to move towards the exit.

'But we have no way of contacting him, we're after him too. What coin are you talking about as well?' I said to his back.

'Don't be so silly. You know exactly what I'm talking about. As for finding Clive? Well, you'll just have to try very, very hard, now, Daniel won't you? You've been given one final chance, all of you, I suggest you grab it with both hands while they're still functioning and attached to your arms. Come along, now, Mr Chomp, if we're lucky, that little girl will still be outside playing on the swings. I know how you love to play on the swings.' He left without looking back, but the man mountain stood for a brief moment longer, eyeing up Abby and me as if we were lunch. He nodded his head once more than turned and walked out after Mr Chew.

For a moment, I just sat there staring at the exit, a part of me unable to believe that the meeting had taken place at all. For all I knew, Chomp and Chew could have been figments of my imagination, just like the wind and my dad's voice.

'Oh, my God, what the Hell was that?' It was Abby's voice that convinced me that they were very real.

'I think that's why Clive's gone postal.'

'Do you think they've gone?' she said with a tremble in her voice.

'Yeah, I think so, they've said what they needed to. I don't think they're the kind of people that have to worry about effect.'

'We need to get out of here; we need to get away right now, as far away as we can.'

'And then what? If we do that, they'll go for you mum? They know about you, Abby, we can't keep your mum safe by running away.'

'What do we do, then?'

'Exactly what he said, we chase your brother and we go get the coin. If they have both, they might leave us alone.' I said this without a flicker of emotion. Clive had brought this on all of us and deserved everything he got as far as I was concerned.

'But it's like you said, we don't know where he is.'

'Yeah, but I bet he knows where we are.'

'What do you mean?'

'We figured he was coming here because he's guessing this is here my dad hid the coin, after finding nothing at Paxton House. He must know we're on the island too, we were right behind him. I bet we'll see him pretty quick if we go outside.' I stood up to leave but she remained seated.

'Do you think they're still out there?' Her head shook as she spoke, the whites of her eyes standing out against her golden skin.

'They're not after you, they're after him. We can get out, no bother. The quicker we're away from here and chasing Bluecoat the better you'll feel, I promise.' I was amazed at how calm I felt. We'd just been threatened by two of the most evil men on the planet and yet I felt as cool as a cucumber, I was more concerned about Abby and how she was feeling.

'Why do you call him that? Why do you call him Blue-coat?'

'Because he wears a blue coat.'

'But why not call him Clive?'

'Because he's not Clive to me. He's something else, he's gone beyond being your brother, he's Bluecoat.' I turned

124

and walked away from her before she could ask another question. I didn't want to tell her that he was a monster in my eyes and that monsters didn't deserve names. I walked through the exit from the theatre and hoped she was following, I really didn't want to go back into that hell hole. Half way through the museum, she caught up and took my arm, much to my relief.

'We're going to be okay aren't we?'

'Yeah, we're going to be fine. There's a way out of this, Abby, just trust me.'

She gave me one of those looks again, the ones normally meant to melt my resolve, only this time I was sure it was intended to have to opposite effect.

'Okay, now what do we do?' she asked.

It looked like I was in charge of the chase once again.

19 - A CHASE ACROSS THE BAY

W e walked out into the bright sunlight and stood in confusion for a brief moment, trying to get our bearings in the bright new world.

'Do we just stand here and hope he sees us or do we head somewhere else?'

'We go for the coin, he'll follow us.'

'What do you mean? We haven't found it here or Paxton House. Where else could it be?

I'd really known for a while where the coin was. Deep down in my gut anyway. The realisation had only bubbled to the surface after we'd found nothing in the museum and we'd had the terrifying encounter with Chomp and Chew.

'St Aidan's church.'

'What, back at the castle?'

'Well, near there.'

'That's where it is, are you sure?'

'Yeah, I'm sure.'

'But how sure are you? I don't want to waste time getting there only to find you're wrong. Shouldn't we just go looking for Clive instead?' She walked towards me as she asked her questions, emphasizing them with her eyes.

'It's there, trust me. I'll show you when we get there, and Clive will follow, he has to. I was wrong before, he wasn't only coming here to look for the coin, he was trying to keep that appointment with those two pyromaniacs. He probably thought he could persuade them not to break his legs and give him one more chance instead, the idiot. Looks like we scuppered that one. Besides, I know he'll follow us because he's watching us right now.'

'What!' She turned with a start and began scanning up and down the road.

'No, don't, we don't want to spook him.'

'Have you seen him?' she whispered.

'Yep, I think so.'

'Where is he?'

'That doesn't matter, he's here so let's get going.'

'I don't get it, why would he follow us now, won't he just wait till we've gone and go into the museum?'

'Like I said, I think he was meant to look for the coin and then meet Chomp and Chew but he never showed. Probably because we beat him to the punch by getting into the place before him. He probably went to the priory first, to look for the coin. There was no way he could come and meet them while we were there, that would have been far too dangerous and probably given them hostages. Better to stay away and leave us to it. Even though he had to get here to meet them and look for the coin, he couldn't risk us losing him either, just in case he was wrong about where it was. He needed to keep us as close as he dare in case he still needs me to show him where it is. He's just been far enough in front of us every time but not too far away. When you think about it, he's never really let us lose him, has he? I bet he's really confused now that they've left and we've come out too.'

'I know I am,' interrupted Abby.

'What I mean is, he's probably seen us and the two monsters go into the museum and seen us all come out and we appear to be whole and healthy. He must have guessed those two wouldn't just leave you alone. They've probably warned him that they'll breaking your legs or something if he doesn't get them the coin and here he is a no show and you walk right into that trap and walk straight back out again. I bet he's wondering what the hell's going on. If I was him, I'd be following you right now, so let's go.'

Abby considered my explanation for a moment. 'Hang on what if he thinks we found it and they took it off us?'

'Leaving us on one piece afterwards? No I don't think so. They came out and then we did, all healthy. We didn't find the coin, it's the only reasonable explanation.'

'Yeah that seem fair. Hold on a minute I need to pee,' she said turning back towards the museum entrance.

'Abby!'

'Well! If what you say is right, then he's not going anywhere, is he?'

'Yeah, okay,' I replied with a sigh, 'but be quick.' I stood basking in the hot afternoon sun waiting for her to return, trying my best not to look down the lane at the scrap of blue poking out of the side of a house. After what seemed an age she returned with a bottle of water and a couple of bags of crisps.

'Is he still there?' she asked, handing me a bag of crisps.

'Yeah I think so, I've been trying not to look.'

'What about them, have you seen them?' there was a slight tremble to her lips as she asked.

'No not a sign, they're well gone.'

She seemed satisfied by my answer and not a little relieved. 'Let's head back to the car.'

We walked in silence, just another couple of tourists leaving the island after a pleasant trip. When we got back to the car, Abby grabbed my arm before turning on the engine.

'Is he still there?'

I looked around but all I could see was the cars parked around us. 'No idea. He must be, let's get going.'

Abby turned on the ignition and nothing happened. The car whined and died. She turned the key again and again, but the same dying whine was as she could make the car do.

'The batteries flat, we need help with a jump start.'

'Not a chance,' she replied. 'We can't get into a conversation with anyone, you never know if they'll recognise you. We're so close. We have to avoid the police until we get that coin and stop Clive.'

I knew she was right, but without help there was no way we were going to get the car started. Then an idea struck me. 'We walk; we can take the Pilgrim's Way.'

Abby was about to take another swig of water when the bottle stopped half way to her lips as she considered my answer. 'Are you sure? I thought no one did that anymore?'

'Well, I think some do on religious occasions, and the odd nutter. The route's still there, so we might as well. Once we get off the island it's only a mile or so to the church.'

The Pilgrim's Way was a track from the mainland to the Island. It had been the only way to and from Holy Isle for centuries before they built the causeway. Thousands of pilgrims would follow St Cuthbert's Way, as it was known, over the flat expanse of sand at low tide and finish up at the priory on the island. When the sea was out, the route was fairly straightforward. It was dangerous at high tide however and the odd tourist had lost their life because they forgot to check the tidal times before setting off.

'I'll go back in and ask the girl at the reception if she knows the tidal times.'

'No don't bother, the less of an impression we leave here the better. Besides, I'm sure low tide is the afternoon.'

She looked at me for a moment, trying to gauge my certainty.

'Well okay, if you're sure.' With that simple agreement we got out of the car and set off into the latest pit of hell.

The track to the bay was brief and uneventful. Both of us kept to our thoughts and I desperately tried to stop turning around to see if he was there. It seemed strange for him to be following me for a change. I'd been so used to trying to spot a flash of blue on the horizon that it felt unnatural to stare ahead and see only sea and sky. Abby seemed as jumpy as hot fat on a skillet. I could see it took every ounce of strength she had to keep staring straight ahead. Her legs moved in a jerky fashion, her arms rotated spasmodically as she moved forward and her breathing came out in quick, sharp breaths.

'Calm down, he's there.'

She nodded briefly in reply and her shoulders sagged

slightly, but her movements remained irritated.

'I wasn't sure if he'd seen us leave the car or not.'

We tracked through the sand dunes and came out onto an empty beach. Up ahead, a series of tall thin poles began at the water's edge and stretched away into the bay.

'Okay, there it is and, see, the tide's out. We should make the crossing quickly if we keep up a good pace.'

'What about him? We'll be able to see him as soon as he starts after us, won't he be worried about that? Perhaps we should take the road, Dan; we don't want to lose him?'

'Don't worry, as soon as we're on the sand he has to follow. He won't be worrying about being seen then. Come on, let's get going.' I set off before she could object or change her mind.

The sand, while firm, had been rippled by the tide making it uneven and difficult to walk on. We had to navigate around large areas of standing water, or wade through them, and our shoes quickly became heavy as the salt water soaked through to the skin. Abby's breathing became laboured as she strode beside me, her chest heaving in and out with the effort of walking over the uneven terrain. After a particularly difficult stretch, where we had to splash through an ankle deep pool of water, I noticed with increasing concern that the pools we're becoming more and more frequent. Then Abby grabbed me by the arm.

'Dan, the sand's disappeared; I think the tide's coming in.'

I scanned around me for the first time and noticed a large expanse of silver water nearly all around us, sparkling in the afternoon light.

'Okay, we're about halfway across. We need to keep up this pace and we'll be over before the tide comes in.'

'What about him? He's behind us now.'

'What about him?' I asked with a shrug. 'He's on his own, come on let's get going.' Any more delays and we would be toast. Our only option was to keep moving and hope the tide didn't come in too quickly.

'That's everyone's mistake, Dan, the tide comes in at speed, you have to pick up the pace.' For once my dad talked sense and I increased my strides, splashing down as I went, my strength slowly sapping away with each step. I could hear Abby's harsh breaths become more frequent as the pace increased. Then she screamed. I turned to see her falling down into the cold water, her hands disappearing below the surface as she attempted to break her fall. She stayed there on her hands and knees, cursing the sky, the sea and the sand until I knelt down and picked her up.

'Are you okay?' I asked.

'Yeah, I stood in a hole, be careful it's getting really treacherous.'

'We need to get across as quickly as we can; can you go any faster?'

She stared at me with a withering look then nodded. 'Just as long as you can keep up big boy.'

'I'm sure I can,' I replied, laughing. 'Come on, let's get out of here.'

The water was now above our ankles. Every movement felt like we were ploughing through ice cold treacle; a strange feeling for a hot summer's afternoon. The effort of lifting a leg and plopping it down into the sea became more and more difficult. To my horror, the water seemed to rise with every step, first above my ankle, then up my calf, then washing around my knees. I turned to look at Abby and check on how she was doing, taking a stride forward as I did and the world toppled over and I fell into hell.

The cold enveloped me in an icy embrace as I plunged under the water. The breath froze in my lungs, my skin screamed in pain as a thousand tiny daggers pierced it and my clothes became a suit of lead pulling me down into the cold depths. The world spun on its axis as I descended, a kaleidoscope of dark greys, blacks and blues spinning across my vision. I expected to feel the sea bed quickly and lurched down in terror without connecting with the bottom, my arms flailing, my legs kicking around me. I hit the bottom with my rear and the remaining breath was pushed out of my lungs. My arms reached out and connected with the sides of a wall of sand and I realized with mounting terror that I'd fallen into some kind of hole. Trying to grab at the sea and sand around me I vainly attempted to gain some momentum upwards as my lungs began to burn. My clothes flailed and whipped over me, catching my arms and pulling me down. Eventually, I managed to get my feet onto the sandy bottom and pushed with my remaining strength. I shot upwards and broke the surface of the water, screaming and coughing as I did. I drew in a deep breath then disappeared below the surface before bobbing up once more. Still coughing and spluttering I felt around for the lip of the hole and grabbed onto the edge with relief. The waves were now washing over my head, sending me below the surface every time they did. My mouth filled with sea water, bitter and acrid, while my body was washed around the side of the hole. I didn't have the strength to haul myself out of the trap and looked around desperately for Abby. She was standing a few metres away, silent and stoic, staring at my desperate attempts to survive.

'Help me!' I spluttered, before disappearing below the surface once again.

She took a step forward as I broke the surface once again, then stopped and continued to stare.

'Abby, please!' I gurgled, sea water streaming out of my mouth. My fingers dug into the side of the hole as I tried to haul myself out but my left leg was caught on a root hidden within the depths of the death trap and my body began to pull me down once more. 'Help me!' I screamed in desperation.

She waded forward but stopped before she got too close. 'I can't. I'm sorry, you don't understand. I have to do everything I can, you would too, I'm so sorry, Dan.'

With that she turned on her heels and plunged for the shore line. I watched her go in utter disbelief. This was my friend, my girlfriend, my best friend for years. We'd played on the swings together, shared ice creams and meaningless secrets, we'd even shared a first kiss. Here she was, wading away as fast as her legs could carry her, leaving me to drown in a deep and dark oubliette.

'Oohhh, very clever, Dan, an oubliette, a dark place where you'd leave someone to rot. I bet the crabs would get you long before then, Danny boy.' The wind chuckled as it brushed over my soaking head and grabbed the back of my neck with its icy fingers.

'Abby!' I screamed once more before disappearing beneath the waves. The sea took me in its cold embrace once again. My remaining strength flooded out of me, my arms turned to lead pipes and my legs refused to move. I was plunging into the darkness, the chase finally over, nothing left to give.

'I'm going to die, Dad, I'm going to be meeting you soon. I hope you'll forgive me for letting you down, I couldn't help it?'

A blue haze fell across my vision as my lungs started to complain about the lack of air. Shapes danced and twirled in front of me, becoming solid then bursting into fireworks of brilliant blue. One by one they began to coalesce, becoming solid form then turning from blue to green to brown. After a moment I could see honey coloured ears of corn whisper across my view, Abby stood in the centre of them, beckoning me forward. She looked awesome in a bright blue summer dress, her hair falling around her shoulders and provocatively hiding most of her face. A knowing smile was etched across the half of her red, moist mouth visible through the golden strands of hair. Her arms were raised in welcome, pulling me forward, inviting me into her embrace.

'It's all here, Dan, all the answers to every question you could ever ask. Just come forward and I'll give them to you. Just come forward and let me hold you, that's all you need to do, it's easy.' I tried to raise my arms but they wouldn't move, I tried to speak but my mouth just filled with salt water once again.

'Look up, Danny, look up.' My dad's voice echoed in my head, soft and firm. I tilted my head upwards and saw a face staring back at me from above the glassy surface of the sea. The eyes wobbled through the surface, the mouth and nose waving in and out of focus.

Arms stretched towards the glass and the surface smashed apart as strong hands grabbed the shoulders of my jacket. I felt the water rush around me as I shot upwards and managed to draw in a feeble breath as my body broke the surface of the sea and returned to the freezing cold day. I coughed and spluttered and managed to take in another deeper breath. More coughing racked my body and spewed water out of my mouth, then I was moving forward as Abby began to drag my body up and out of the hole and headed towards the shore. I shook with fear and fatigue, my arms and shoulders rattling inside my sodden clothes and my teeth chattering against each other.

For what seemed an age, I only knew cold and pain and the constant churning of the sea. The hands never left my shoulders, half dragging, half pushing me across the flooded bay. My legs fell up and down in a spasmodic attempt to walk, my arms flailed at my sides. Each breath I took was raw and painful, sending cold, moist air deep into my lungs. If there was a hell, this was it. Each movement was pain, each step towards safety a delicious agony. I wanted to speak, to thank Abby for coming back for me and to chastise her for leaving in the first place but I couldn't. Sound was a luxury I couldn't afford, so I kept my eyes cast down at my feet, fixed on their motion, watching them plod in and out of the water in erratic fashion. I focused on staying upright and concentrated on trying to ignore the pain and cold surrounding me. I could thank her as soon as I was out I told myself, thank her and slap her too.

'You must never, ever, ever hit a lady, Dan; that's unforgivable.'

'Yeah well so is leaving someone to die, Dad.'

After an age, my steps became easier as the level of the water became lower and before I realized it we were walking on solid ground. The hand left my shoulders and I gratefully collapsed onto soft warm sand. My body sang with aches and shivered in the cold but I could feel the sun on my face and dry sand beneath my finger tips and knew that I was going to be okay. I'd made it, I'd gone through yet another level of hell and come out the other side.

After a time, my breathing slowed and the shaking lessened. My clothes still felt heavy and cold around me, and my joints ached from the attempts I'd made to get out of the hole, but this was so familiar to me now that it took just a few seconds of listening to my body to know I was going to be able to continue. After a few moments, I finally felt able to speak and lifted my head to thank her for saving me when Clive's beaten and weathered face came into view.

'Are you okay?' he asked through gasps. 'That was a close one, I thought you'd disappeared down that hole for good.'

At first I couldn't understand why he was asking me this or why he was laid out beside me gasping for breath. He should have been back in the bay swimming for his life, yet here he was asking stupid questions he had no right to ask. Then it hit me, Abby hadn't come back; Clive had saved me from drowning. She'd left me to die after all; if it hadn't been for him I'd be swimming with the fishes right now.

20 - THE CUSTARD-COLOURED SIGN

'Why did you save me?' I croaked.

'Because I'm no monster, Dan, whatever you may think.'

'Oh, my God, she left me. She left me out there to die. I think it's your sister who's the monster.'

'We all have a demon inside us, Dan, even Abby.'

The reality of what just happened struck me like a hammer blow. She'd left me as soon as she could, and not in a safe warm place, either. In a cold wet grave. What was worse is that I shouldn't have been the least bit surprised. It was what Abby did. She got what she wanted and never gave a thought for the trail of destruction she left in her wake. This time, she clearly wanted the coin. The devastation left over from her attempts to get it were left on my battered body.

Clive leaned over with a groan and lay flat on the sand. I was too dumbstruck to think properly. The monster, the killer I'd been chasing all this time had now turned out to be my saviour while my best friend and the crutch I'd used to get me through had turned into the monster. The world made no sense. I lay back on the sand and looked up at the arc of blue above me. The single cloud had disappeared, re-placed by a thin line of white cloud running across the horizon.

'This is such a beautiful place, why did we make it so ugly?'

He leaned over on his side and looked at me. 'Because it's what men do. We're all ugly inside and it makes us want to destroy the beauty around us. That's how it's been for me anyway.'

'I think we just can't stop and appreciate it all, that's our problem. It would be really nice to stop and smell the flowers for a change, do you know what I mean?'

'Yeah I know exactly what you mean, my God, I do.'

We lay there for a few more moments in silence and I gradually began to feel normal again, or as normal as you can be after yet another near death experience, particularly one that leaves you soaked to the skin.

'What now?' I asked reluctantly. I couldn't believe I was having this conversation with him, I couldn't believe I was being civil to him at all, but he had saved my life and there was no way we could lie there forever.

'You met them didn't you? You met Chomp and Chew?'

I nodded in reply.

'Then you know I have no choice. I need to go on. I need to get the coin. You can try and stop me, you can phone the police, but I need to go on. You must realize that after meeting them?'

Reluctantly I nodded in reply once again. I'd met them and experienced the terror of their presence. I fully understood why Clive was doing what he was doing and I now knew he needed to keep on doing it until the monsters were satisfied. It didn't excuse him or his actions. There would have to be a reckoning, but I knew it wasn't going to be right now, however much I wanted it to be.

'Has she gone after it, Dan?'

'Yeah, she knows where it is. I guess she was just waiting for me to tell her before she ditched me. She certainly picked her time to do that. I just don't understand why. We were going for it together, so why leave me to die?'

'I don't know. Maybe meeting Chomp and Chew freaked her out and she panicked? Maybe finding out what I did to my dad tipped her over the edge, who knows? I don't think she stopped to think about it, though; she's not a murderer, Dan.'

'No she only goes for attempted murder. You weren't there, you didn't see her eyes.'

'No you're right, I didn't. Where's she going?'

I realized he was the only one of our little group who still didn't know where the coin was, it had been the one thing keeping us in the chase, even though I didn't know it till late in the day, and now he was going to find out where his prize was simply by asking. If only he'd been honest with me a lot earlier, we might have saved ourselves a lot of heartache.

'It's hidden in St Aidan's church.' He nodded then turned and lay back down. I'd half expected him to jump up and begin running towards the church, or to stand up and demand to get going at least. This was what he'd been after all along, he now had his answer, so why not go after it as fast as his legs could carry him?

'What are you doing, I thought you wanted to go after the coin?'

He didn't reply for a long while, then, just before I was sure he wasn't going to, he turned over onto his side and looked at me. 'That damn thing has cost me everything. My family, my livelihood, my safety, my future. I'm in no rush to give it the rest of me just yet.'

'And you cost me my dad.' I said this without malice or anger; it was just a statement of fact.

He looked at me for a long time before replying. 'Yeah, I did and I'm sorry, I really am. I'm going to pay for that I know, but not before I get Abby to safety.' He finally stood up and brushed himself off. She might have been a monster but she was still his sister and he wanted to keep her safe. Like her, he was even willing to forgive murder (or attempted murder in Abby's case), if it meant keeping his sibling safe. 'Stay here and rest, you look like you've been pulled through a hedge backwards. I'll go after her now, you've been through enough.'

'No chance,' I replied quickly. 'I let you go then you disappear over the horizon, it isn't happening.' The thought of letting him go even after he saved my life sent shivers down my spine.

He looked down at me for a moment them nodded with a sigh.

'Are you sure that's the only reason? You just want to keep Abby safe? I thought you needed the coin to get them off your back?' I asked.

'I keep her safe by getting them off my back. Do you think they only threatened me? They made it very clear that my whole family was in danger if I didn't get them what they wanted. Yeah, this is all my fault, I know that, I've put everyone in danger, I've cost lives. But that doesn't mean I don't want to protect people too. It doesn't mean I don't love my sister and want to keep her from danger.

'What?' I shouted at him in disbelief. 'You threatened to shoot her this morning; how is that keeping her safe?'

'You don't understand,' he replied, spreading his fingers wide in an attempt to calm me down. 'I would never intentionally try to harm her and I only meant to scare you both in the café. I just needed to get away from you so I could check out the priory and museum on the island and meet those two without you being there. I was in a desperate situation, Dan; hell I'm still in it, don't you see? I'm just trying to get out of this the best way I can.'

'And that means killing people, Clive, don't you see that?' I bunched my hands into balls and felt the anger stew inside me. I'd been too fatigued to care about anything just moments before but his comments had got my blood boiling.

'I can never go back and stop that from happening, but you know I would if I could. Like I said, I'll pay for that, I need to get the coin, then you can get your revenge right after it's in their hands and Abby's safe. It's the best I can do right now.'

My anger flooded away like water down a drain. However much I hated him, I knew what he was saying was right and foolishly I still wanted to help Abby, too. Even after what she'd done. Perhaps we were more alike than I would like to admit.

'Okay, I'll go with you now, but it's the cells right afterwards, for you and for Abby.'

He considered this for a moment then nodded his head in agreement. 'Okay. How far is it to the church from here?'

'Not far,' I replied, standing up with a groan. 'We can take St Oswald's way, it'll get us there pretty quickly.'

'Does Abby know that way too?'

'Yeah, probably better than I do.'

'Then we better get going; which way?' I pointed to a sign at the end of the beach, half hidden by a fir tree.

'That's the start of it over there.'

We made our way to the sign over soft sand still radiating heat from the warm day. I soon began to feel my joints ease in the heat but my clothes had become a tight, cloying blanket wrapped around me. I stripped off my heavy jacket as we walked and let it drop to the sand. I briefly thought about getting rid of my wet trousers too but dismissed it with a smirk; Abby would go wild if I did.

Oswald's way was a popular walk linking the Holy Island to Hadrian's Wall in the south. The route was named after King Oswald, later made a saint, who ruled over the place in the seventh century. The route hugs the coast before heading inland but we weren't going to follow it that far. Luckily for us, it passed right by our destination and I was hoping we'd be able to follow it without incident and be there soon.

'St Oswald was a great king of Northumbria, Dan, he united the kingdoms and helped spread Christianity. If it wasn't for him, St Aidan wouldn't have come to the country and we wouldn't be visiting his church right now. Do you know, Oswald's right arm is kept in a casket in the church, Dan?'

'Yeah, Dad, I know, it's the reason we're going there,' I replied under my breath.

'But of course it is, you're such a clever chap, Dan. I'm really proud of you, did I ever tell you that?'

'No, you bloody didn't, and that was the point. Pity it takes death and insanity for you to say it, Dad.' He didn't reply but Clive turned around at my mumblings.

'You okay?'

'Yeah I'm fine, just checking my joints.'

'Is this the right way?'

'Yeah, all we have to do is follow the path, it takes us right past the church.'

We made our way down the path as it meandered in and out of a small copse of trees and over the odd sand dune. Eventually, it snaked further in land and levelled off to a narrow rutted outline of hard earth, its borders scattered with wild flowers and weeds. We walked in silence, the soft breeze and the twitter of birds the only sounds accompanying us.

I looked up and beyond Clive every now and again, not sure what colours I was looking for. I remembered Abby wearing a denim jacket at one time during the morning but after that I wasn't sure. It seemed strange to think of her before us, running as fast as she could towards the church. I wondered if she was in a panic, running away from her actions as much as running towards Clive's salvation, but somehow I didn't think so. I understood why she'd done what she had, at least I hoped I did. A big part of me wanted to believe she had acted rashly so she could help her brother. A small voice niggled at the back of my mind, however, telling me she'd known what she was doing and had planned to ditch me all along. The drowning in a pit of hell had just been a bonus. A strange calm fell over me as we walked. I knew where I was and accepted why I was there. I didn't feel a need to chase, to race forward, to catch a glimpse of blue. The fact that the chase had turned from Clive to Abby hadn't altered my feelings. The hole still felt full and I could have happily turned around there and then and walked off into the sunset. It was curiosity more than anything which kept me walking. I wanted to hear Abby's explanation and see if Clive had been right about her losing it.

A large, bright metal cylinder came into view as we turned a corner. It was easily twenty metres high and sported a conical top. Another was nestled not far away and half a dozen more sat in the background. Over the top of the one closest to us was a custard coloured sign proudly proclaiming 'Northern Granary Co' in letters a metre high. It wasn't the cylinders that held Clive's attention however. Abby was quickly disappearing around the side of the one closest to us.

'There she is!' he shouted striding forward to chase after her. I followed closely behind, watching his bright blue coat rattle over his back as he ran. The irony of the situation wasn't lost on me. I was chasing him as he chased her. The gods have a delicious sense of humour, it would seem.

We entered the forest of metal cylinders and skidded to a halt on the gravel path surrounding them. Clive swung on his heels, looking this way and that, desperately trying to find his sister. I just stood there and listened. After a few moments, a scuffling sound and movement off to my left drew my attention; she was getting away.

'Clive, over here!'

We raced after her, our boots crunching into the gravel below us, sending chips rattling off the nearest cylinder. After a moment she came into view striding towards the centre of the granary.

'Abby, stop!' Clive shouted. 'Stop, it's okay!'

She swivelled around to look at us and lost her footing, falling to a crumpled heap at the base of a tower. We raced forward and were met by the tip of a black cylinder wobbling uncertainly from her outstretched hand.

'Stay away, I'll use it!' she squawked.

We both skidded to a halt, our hands raised instinctively.

'Oh, my God, Abby, what the hell are you doing? Where did you get the gun?' I said uncertainly.

'Never mind where I got the gun, just leave right now.'

'Abby, what are you doing? Don't be a fool, we're here to help,' Clive said softly.

'Here to help,' she laughed. 'It's me that's been helping you, you idiot, don't you remember?'

'Yes of course I do,' Clive replied with a quick glance in my direction, 'but there's no need to point a gun, Abby, we're not here to harm you,' he said softly as he took a tentative step forward.

'What do you mean you've been helping him?' I asked, but Abby ignored me, all her focus on her brother.

'You're not here to harm me? You couldn't harm a fly

could you Clive? Oh, and Dan here will be okay with the fact that I left him to drown, we're all friends then are we?'

'I know you didn't mean it, Abby,' I said softly.

'Of course I bloody meant it, you moron! Just like I meant to find you in the castle, and just like I meant to take you back to my hotel room and keep you safe. Just like I meant to take you to Paxton House and just like I meant you to meet him there. It's been me all along, I can't believe you never guessed it. I was meant to be with you, Danny, I've been keeping you safe ever since we met. I had to, it was the only way I could be sure this idiot brother of mine didn't mess it. I knew you were the only one who had even the slightest idea where your dad hid that coin. Don't you see, keeping you close kept the coin close? My God, I managed to ditch you as soon as you told me where it definitely was. That should have been some sort of clue.'

Her venom washed over me and stung my heart. This was a new Abby, one I'd only seen glimpses of before. She was as hard as steel with cold grey eyes to match. There was no warmth to her and only razor sharp edges. I could see nothing but contempt written across her face, for me and for her brother.

'You knew, all along? You knew about Clive, and the trouble he was in? You knew about Chomp and Chew?'

'Of course I knew, he tells me everything, he always has. I'm the only one who will talk to him most of the time anyway. Why wouldn't I know my brother?'

I looked at them both in turn. Abby sat against the cylinder her eyes blazing, her hand wobbling out in front of her. Clive stood at my side, head down, eyes gazing intently at the gravel. Suddenly it all made sense. He was the idiot, the black sheep, but she was the manipulator, the calculating sister. Always willing to do anything to keep her brother safe. They'd been playing me all this time.

'Abby, did you know about your dad before he told you in the cafe?'

'No I didn't know that,' she replied softly.

'But why go to all that trouble? If you wanted to know where the coin was, all you had to do was ask?'

'Because it's that easy,' she replied with a sneer. 'Where's that gold coin people are dying over, Danny boy? That's all I needed to ask? Turns out you really didn't know about the coin until we met Clive in the cafe. I had to keep you close while we searched the museum and I was right to, it wasn't there either. But I knew you were right as soon as you mentioned St Aidan's church. '

My mind reeled with her revelations. She'd been pulling her brother's strings all along. He may have done the deed, but Abby was dictating the play that much was obvious from her admissions. But how much had she really manipulated events since the sorry tale had all begun?

'So, you knew everything from the beginning, then? Your loser of a brother came to you begging for help. He'd got himself in a spot of bother, is that right?' She licked her lips before replying.

'He told me everything just after mum got sick. That lot he told you back at the café, Dan that much was true.'

'And you've been helping him ever since?'

'Yeah.'

'But he kept the fact he killed you dad from you didn't he?'

'Abby, we need to go,' Clive stepped forward and reached out for the gun.

'Get the hell away from me!' she screamed, stopping him in his tracks. 'You and me we were finished the second you told me you caused my dad's heart attack, brother dearest. I'll get your damn coin for you; after that you're on your own. Until then, keep your distance.'

He stepped back with his arms raised, nodding slowly as he went.

She turned to me with tears rolling down her face. 'I knew about your dad as soon as it happened,' she answered in a voice just above a whisper.

'Abby, no!' Clive hissed through clenched teeth.

'Clive was running away and I was chasing him. How the hell did you know so soon?' the answer exploded in my brain before she could reply. 'Because you were there weren't you? Back in the B&B, you said my dad was going to meet someone and it must have been Clive. But I never told you he was going to meet anyone. All I told you was that he'd been shot by your brother. I should have guessed it then. Come to think of it you knew about his death when I met you in the castle, but his identity still hadn't been released by the police, so there's no way you could have known, without some inside knowledge, isn't that right?'

She nodded in reply, her eyes downcast, tears dripping from her nose and dropping one by one onto the gravel.

My knees buckled beneath me and I crumpled to the floor. But my eyes never left her sobbing body. Her face hidden behind a vale of honey coloured hair. She'd known all along. She'd known when we met in the King's Hall, she'd known when we risked our lives climbing over the castle walls and she'd known when we raced across the bay being chased by the tide.

'You knew all this time? You never saw the news like you said when we first met did you? You didn't need to, you had a front row seat to the whole thing. How come I never saw you there?'

'It's a long dark tunnel and there's an exit on the other side. I left as soon as I could.'

I shook my head and sighed. 'You can add leaving the scene of a murder to everything else you've done, then!' I spat at her.

She lifted her face and stared at me with her flint coloured eyes, heat slowly rising in her cheeks. 'All my crimes? Oh I'm guilty of so much aren't I? I'm guilty of loving and protecting my brother. I'm guilty of trying to keep what's left of my family together and I'm guilty of trying to do the right thing. Oh, yeah, I'm guilty of a great many crimes.'

'You let him kill my dad and then you lied about it!' I screamed, hot and sour bile spilling into my throat.

'I had no choice!' She screamed in reply.

'You had every choice,' I replied, cold fury sinking into the pit of my stomach. 'You let it happen and then you lied about it to keep your brother safe. You didn't go to the cops like a normal person. You didn't tell me. Instead you covered it up and pretended you didn't know he'd done it. You're worse than him, he's a monster but he never intended to kill anyone. You knew about it all and did nothing. No, you did worse than nothing; you did everything you could to make matters worse. You're a new kind of monster, I don't think they even have a name for you.'

She dug her free hand into the gravel and pushed herself up. Her face a mask of rage and hurt, her eyes blazed with fury, no doubt reflecting the anger in mine. 'I'm a monster, am I?' she said, levelling the gun at my forehead. 'If I'm a monster like you say, I can just pull the trigger and walk away then, can't I? After all, I don't need you anymore. I know where the coin is, so you're useless now, you're just a bag of bones and blood. That's what a monster would think anyway.'

'Go on, then, do it. You never gave me a second thought when you left me to drown, so why hesitate now? Go on, monster, pull the trigger!'

Her gun hand wavered for a moment, her grip white on the handle, a myriad thoughts flashing across her face. Then slowly she lowered her hand to her side. 'That's what you'd want me to do isn't it? You'd want me to be that monster, but you're wrong. I'm no more a monster than you. A son who'd leave his father lying in the road, bleeding to death.'

My rage exploded out of me, pushing me up and towards her, my hands reaching for her. 'He was dead, you bitch!' I scrambled over her outstretched arms, my fingers desperately seeking her throat. Clive grabbed me from behind, pulling with all his strength, trying to get me away from his sister. We wrestled for a moment, one massive beast, hot and close, all arms and legs, spit and sweat spraying around us. Then Clive got a grip under my armpits and hauled me to the ground with all his strength. I lay there for a moment then rose to my haunches, looking up at them both with unconcealed loathing.

'He was dead and your bastard of a brother killed him. I'm going to kill you both for that. I'm going to dance over your corpses!'

'You're the monster, Dan, you're the beast, look at the

146

way you're acting. You're no grieving son, you love it! You wanted this, you wanted the chase,' she replied, spitting the words at me with all the venom she could muster.

'I wanted none of this. I had to go after your brother. He killed him!' I yelled at the top of my voice.

'I killed him!' She screamed at me, staggering backwards and hitting the silver cylinder. She leant there for a moment, panting like a dog, her eyes wide, and her gun hand trembling. 'I killed him, it was me. I'm the one you should hate,' she said quietly.

My whole body went numb as I desperately tried to understand what she'd just said.

'What?' I replied pathetically.

'Don't say anything else,' Clive hissed.

She shook her head in reply. 'He has to know, everyone needs to know. It was me in the alley, Dan, I wrestled with your dad. I didn't mean to shoot him, my God, you have to know that, he just wouldn't let go. He kept hissing at me. Telling me how disappointed my dad would have been. He went on and on and wouldn't let go. I had to make him let go.' She lowered her head into her hands and began to sob deeply.

I watched her crumple into a sobbing ball from a million miles away. The whole experience was happening to another Dan. A haunted empty Dan, with no life left in him. I saw Clive slowly move forward, lean down and place a hand tenderly onto his sister's back. I saw her resist for a moment then lean into his bent body, her head resting on his chest. I turned away from them slowly and looked up at the top of the tower stretching away from me and touching the sky.

Before I knew it, I was laid flat on the hard gravel, staring at the sky, hoping to see my lonely cloud one last time. While I lay there I tried not to see her wrestling with my dad. I tried not to hear her warn him to let go. I screwed my eyes shut when the sound of the gun going off pierced my ears. I looked away when my dad staggered away from her, blood pouring out of his body. I could hear her gasp at the realisation of what she'd done and saw her turn around and race away, leaving him for dead.

I opened my eyes and I was back in my body, the cylinder still reaching for the sky in front of me, the brother and sister still locked in a desperate embrace, her sobs racking her body and making them both rock back and forth together.

I considered diving over them while they were distracted and imagined pounding their heads together and burying their bodies in the cold hard ground. But I was in no shape for a fight with the both of them and Abby still held the gun. So I just lay there and watched as Clive slowly brushed the back of Abby's head, whispering into her ear as he did. They'd been a couple all along, a twisted kind of Bonny and Clyde. A sick brother and sister act willing to do anything to get what they want and they'd been playing me from the beginning. Then it stuck me; they'd been playing my dad long before then. He wouldn't have been expecting Abby in that alley. I was guessing he'd been dealing with Clive all along. Abby had kept to the shadows until she had to come out and confront him.

'Why you?' I asked. 'Why did you meet my dad and not Clive?'

There was a pause and a sob before she replied. 'Your dad had been giving my brother the run around, so we figured he'd be shocked to see I was involved. Well, shocked enough to tell me what he wouldn't tell Clive, anyway.'

'You really didn't know him,' I replied dismissively. Once he'd set his mind to it nothing would sway him, and he'd promised Abby's dad he'd keep the coin safe. Not even the threat of being shot could persuade him to spill the beans it would seem. Abby had been wasting her time.

'When that didn't work, you moved onto the son, then, is that it?'

'Like I said before, we figured you might know about it and if you didn't, we might be able to figure it out. It was worth a shot anyway,' Clive replied.

'Yeah, it was definitely worth one shot at least, or quite a few shots as it turned out, hey, Clive? You two are really fond of trying to shoot people aren't you?'

'I've only done what I needed to, I've already explained this,' he replied, continuing to stroke Abby's hair as he did so.

'And you've been speaking to each other all this time, haven't you?'

'What?' Clive replied, looking over at me.

'You've been talking to each other all this time. On the phone, I mean. After all, it makes sense that you would. Otherwise you would never have known to meet us at Paxton House or to go to Holy Isle afterwards? Did she phone you from the museum too to tell you I'd finally spilled the beans about the coin? I bet she did and I bet that was a hard call after you'd said you were going to shoot her? It's a wonder she phoned you at all. So many things didn't make sense before. The way you always kept me close but just far enough away to stop me from catching you. The way Abby just turned up and seemed to accept that you had shot my dad. The way she was so keen to keep me close. Yeah it all makes sense now.'

Clive looked over at me from above Abby's sobbing figure and nodded slowly in reply.

'I thought as much, it all fits. Why wouldn't you work together? You're family, after all. A lying, murdering one, but family nonetheless. You deserve each other.' I stood up slowly and brushed myself down. My body trembled from head to toe. A wave of dizziness washed over me as I stretched and for a moment I thought I was going to fall. Then the world righted itself and the feeling subsided.

'What are you doing, Dan?' Clive asked.

'I should rip you both apart with my bare hands but I'm better than that. So I'm going to walk to the nearest police station and tell them all about it. I think they'll be really interested, don't you? Oh, and good luck finding the coin before the cops arrive. You know it's in the church but you don't know exactly where and my dad was very good at keeping things hidden.'

'You are going nowhere!' Abby spat at me, detaching herself from Clive and wiping tears and snot from her face. She stood up with the gun pointed at my heart. 'Do you think I've been through all this so you can stop me now? I'm going to find that coin. I'm going to leave right now and take a nice walk to the church and then I'm going to rip it apart until I find it.'

'That's fine, go ahead and the police will be waiting for you when you arrive,' I replied with a sneer.

'Oh no that's not going to happen. You and Clive are coming with me.' She waved her gun at us both, then pointed back in the direction of Oswald's Way.

'And then what? You heard those two maniacs earlier; Clive isn't going to meet them until tomorrow. What are you going to do until then? You don't have a car and I'm going to be a very difficult hostage.'

'We all have mobiles. You just said you'd guessed that one already. Clive's already phoned them and arranged to meet them there. We need to get them off our backs as soon as possible, we can't wait any longer. The police might catch up with you and Clive any minute. We agreed that when I went back into the museum to get the drinks and have a pee. My God, Dan, you really need to keep up'

'So it would seem,' I replied with a sigh. There was nothing I could do. Abby held all the cards, not to mention the gun. I was half tempted to run and see if she would follow through on her threat, but this was Abby, not Clive. If she said she was going to shoot me, then she'd do it. There was nothing for it; I had to go along with her, for now.

'Well, seems like you've got everything figured out. Lead on, let's go and get this bloody coin so I can be shot of the both of you once and for all.'

'A very apt turn of phrase, Dan,' she said, waving her gun at me as she walk past.

21 - OSWALD'S RIGHT ARM

We walked in silence for a while, Clive in the lead, then me, then Abby. A thousand questions raced through my mind but Abby pushed the point of her gun into the small of my back every time I tried to turn around to ask them.

We met the odd tourist group every now and again, each one dressed in an array of brightly coloured anoraks, the guide huffing and puffing as they explained points of interest along the route. Abby drew close as each one appeared and warned me to keep quiet with a quick stab of her gun into my back. Eventually, a small town appeared on the horizon, the majestic castle we visited just the day before sat brooding over it on a plateau to the south. I half expected to see smoke still rising from it, but all seemed quiet. In front of us, at the northern edge of the village, a steeple was just visible above the tops of the trees. Clive stopped to catch his breath and pointed to the steeple in the distance.

'Is that St. Aidan's?'

'Yeah that's it.'

'Not long now. You'll be rid of us soon, Dan,' Abby said from behind, giving my back another push with her gun.

'Where the hell did you get that thing?' I asked gruffly, the small of my back aching where she'd pushed it.

'Where do you think, from Clive of course?'

'But how?' I asked, stopping and turning around to face her.

'I've always had it, ever since we planned to meet your dad. We both have one. It's a dangerous world, Dan, you really should never leave home without one.'

'You had a gun all this time?'

'Yes,' she replied blankly.

I shook my head and turned away from her. 'I really don't know you at all.'

'No you don't,' she replied, giving my back another shove.

'One thing I'm curious about though. Clive, how did you know that I would follow you when Abby shot my dad?'

'I didn't. I just started running and you followed. Before I knew it, you were chasing me across the countryside. I phoned Abby as soon as I could and she said keep you close. That you might know something now we couldn't get the info from your dad. That's why I kept going. Why I had to make sure you followed me.'

In a strange, twisted way, their logic made sense. Any normal person would have gone straight to the police, but I hadn't. I'd chased after what I'd thought was my dad's murderer. If only I'd just done the right thing. Then again, I wouldn't have expose their little conspiracy if I had.

St. Aidan's church sat quietly on the edge of town, away from the rattle and hum of tourists heading for the castle. Now we were much closer, I could clearly see the castle's light grey walls and the luxurious tall windows of the King's Hall. I half expected to see smoke still gloating into the air from the burnt out truck, but nothing appeared on the horizon.

'Do you know this has been a place of worship since 635, Dan? Nothing of the original wooden church has survived, unfortunately, except perhaps a wooden beam in the baptistry. Although I'm not convinced of that. The legend has it that St Aidan was leaning against it when he died and that it has miraculously survived two big fires since. I don't know about that, do you?'

'Can it, Dad,' I whispered, taking my eyes off the castle and concentrating on the church instead. The current church was made of light brown and grey stone, with an elegant archway entrance and a squat square bell tower in the centre. From afar, it gave the impression of being a castle rather than a church, but the elegant stained glass windows either side of the entrance soon told you otherwise. We walked up to the entrance through an ancient graveyard full of weatherworn headstones. I hoped that the place was closed to the public, but Clive turned the big round handle easily and the door swung open with a creak.

The interior was cool and dim and from what I could see, empty of any tourists. Large wooden pews occupied the space at the centre, stretching in and out of vision behind a row of thick brown columns. The light was fractured into a warm array of colours as the sun passed through the stained glass windows on either side of the building, splashing rainbows across the pews and over the stone floor. It was a place of peace and serenity. A place you would visit to consider the universe, or try to find inner calm. Or at least it had been until we arrived.

'Where is it?' she asked slowly.

'Why should I tell you? After all you don't need me now. I'm just a bag of blood and bones,' I replied spitefully.

She stood silently for a moment looking at me intently, then slowly walked over and pressed her hand over my heart.

'Do you remember the story of the Green Lady?'

'What on earth are you going on about?'

'The Green Lady, surely your dad told you that one? It's one of the things the castle is famous far, apart from the Beast.'

'Yes he told me the story, what of it?'

She turned away and walked over to one of the hard pews, sitting down with a sigh. 'My dad use to tell me the story all the time when I was little, it was one of my favourites. I cried at the end every time. The Green Lady was the young wife of the lord of the castle up on the hill out there. She was said to be the greatest beauty of her age, so beautiful that a nearby duke coveted her above all things. He tried to seduce her every time he was invited to the castle by her husband, but the lady never told her husband about the unwanted advances for fear of what her lord might do. The duke had the ear of the king you see and any attack on him would be seen as an attack on the king.

'Then, one day, after she had spurned the duke's advances once again, he vowed revenge on her and all her family. He wrote to the king and told him that he had found evidenced proving that the lord was plotting treason against him. The king believed the duke and laid siege to the great castle. The duke was an evil, loathsome man, you understand, and he offered the lady one last chance; the siege would be lifted if she slept with him. The lady would not stain her honour and convinced her lord to offer her one and only son to the king as proof of his loyalty to the crown instead. The king accepted the child as captive but the duke stabbed him to death while he was sleeping, as revenge for the lady's rejection of him.

'The lady was so struck with grief when she found out her only son had been murdered that she flung herself off the battlements. They say she haunts the castle to this day, desperately trying to find her son and husband; he'd been poisoned by the duke shortly after she killed herself.' She looked up at me with a single tear trickling down her face and shrugged. 'I guess it still makes me cry,' she said.

'All very touching but what has it got to do with the coin?'

'Nothing, I guess, I just like the story. I feel for her. She was in a hopeless situation, she couldn't tell her husband and she wouldn't dishonour her marriage vows. She was a real lady,' Abby said quietly. 'She was willing to do almost anything to protect her family. I'm the same, Dan, don't you see?'

'Not really. Like you said, she didn't have options; you did. You could have gone to the police. I'm sure your lady would have if they'd had them back in the day.'

'No, that's not right at all,' she replied, shaking her head. 'She could have gone to her lord but that would have made matters worse, I could have gone to the police and

Clive would be dead now, don't you see? I'm only doing what I have to. I'm sorry you and your dad got caught in the crossfire.'

'Yeah, sure, I'll forgive you. Just as long as you throw yourself off the battlements like your lady did,' I replied, sarcastically.

'Okay,' she said with a sigh. 'You're never going to see it so, fair enough, where's the coin?'

'Like I said, you can find it yourself, you don't need me. I'm just a bag of bones.'

She sighed again and shook her head slowly. 'It's in the casket where Oswald's right arm's supposed to be kept, isn't it.'

'What?' I replied, stunned.

'Oh, come on, Dan, it doesn't take a genius to work that one out. Your dad was an expert on the castle and the only link between the castle and the church is St. Oswald.'

When she put it like that it was obvious.

'So, go and see before the vicar arrives,' Clive said.

She stood up and walked over to a small alcove to the right of the altar. A large ornate wooden box sat on a stand in the recess with a small plaque in front proclaiming this as the last resting place of St Oswald's right arm. St Oswald had been killed in battle and it was said his severed right arm had been reclaimed and brought back to the church as it was supposed to have healing powers. It had been kept in the church ever since as incorruptible evidence of the power of God and thousands of pilgrims had visited over the centuries hoping to be healed of their ailments.

'Far too catholic an idea for the Church of England if you ask me, Dan,' my dad remarked.

'Well no one did, Dad,' I replied under my breath.

Abby knelt in front of the box slowly and raised her hands to the clasp, giving it a brief tug.

'It's locked,' she said.

'Well, of course it is,' Clive replied, shoving her out of the way. He prised the lock open with a small pocket knife, his hands trembling slightly as he did so, then began rummaging inside the box, his face a picture of concentration. After a few moments of searching he brought his hand out with a gasp and held it up so we could see the soft red velvet pouch he held between his fingers.

'Open it up,' Abby said quickly.

Clive drew the draw string slowly then placed his fingers gently inside and retrieved a dull gold coin, holding it up between his fingers triumphantly.

'Doesn't look like much does it? Certainly not shiny enough to cost someone's life,' I said dully.

'It's freedom, Dan, for you and for us. It's the end of the road,' Abby replied, her gaze fixed on the coin held between Clive's grubby fingers.

'Can I see it at least?' I asked, holding out my hand. 'It's cost me my dad, even if you think it's saved your brother.'

She looked at me for a moment, her amazing grey eyes sizing me up once again, then she nodded towards her brother. 'Give it to him, that's the least we can do. But remember, Dan, don't do anything stupid, I've still got the gun.'

'What am I going to do, swallow it?' I replied, taking it from Clive's reluctant fingers. The coin felt small and insignificant in my hands. It had an odd rectangular shape and was slightly bent at one end. The beast itself sat proudly in the centre, its front arms wrapped around it in a complex shape, the rest of its body resting on its hind quarters.

'Looks like a lion or something,' I muttered half to myself.

'It looks like freedom,' Clive replied.

I turned it over and stared at the complex Celtic pattern on the opposite face. A soft contrast to the menacing beast on the other side. Then something at the edge of the coin caught my eye. The chuckle began deep in my belly and slowly rose up through my body before exploding out of my mouth as a roar of laughter.

'Very funny, Dan, now give me the coin,' Abby said dismissively.

I tossed her the coin then doubled over with laughter, my belly aching with the force. My eyes streamed tears, my nose dripped mucus, both pattering to the stone floor beneath my feet. No matter how hard I tried, I couldn't stop. The total futility of the chase hit me with the force of a bomb blast, making me scream with laughter even more. I laughed at the stupidity of the monsters chasing Clive. I laughed at my stupidity for refusing to let Bluecoat go and most of all I laughed at my dad, my arrogant, self-centred, distant dad. After a while the laughter eased and I was able to stand up straight with a groan.

'Better now?' Abby asked, curtly.

'Yeah, much,' I chuckled, 'nice isn't it?' I asked her. 'I especially like the Celtic pattern on the back, very arty.'

'Yeah very,' she replied. 'Either way we won't be looking at it for much longer, they should be here any minute.'

'I wouldn't be too eager to meet them again if I was you,' I said.

'Why not, scared to meet them are you?'

'No, not really, but *you* should be.'

'Oh really, and why is that?' she asked.

'Like I said, it's a really nice Celtic design. I especially like the small print on the side, "Made in China" I think it says,' I spurted out before laughing again.

'What!' Clive shouted. 'Give me that,' he hissed, grabbing the coin from his sister. His face was a mask of concentration for a moment then he gasped, his eyes going wide. 'He's right,' he managed to choke.

Abby grabbed the coin off him and desperately scanned the edge. She found the tiny writing then shivered down the side of the wall, shaking her head from side to side, whispering to herself as she went.

'All for nothing, it's all been for nothing,' Clive whispered to himself, staring off into the middle distance.

'Good evening boys and girls, what a lovely place for a meeting,' a voice said from the back of the church.

22 - A PRAYER FOR THE DYING

I turned around quickly to see Chomp and Chew enter the building. Mr Chew resembled a cat with a mouse caught between its paws. He sported a manic grin under bright murderous eyes as he slunk slowly towards us, his black, shiny shoes shuffling across the stone floor, a dark ebony cane, topped with a bright silver handle, tapping the floor dully as he went. Mr Chomp stood as still as a statue at the door, his arms folded across his massive chest, appearing as impassive as ever.

'I was just saying to Mr Chomp how nice it would be if we were to meet our new young friends again and then we get that lovely phone call from Clive, and here you are with him, not a few hours later. What a lovely surprise, isn't it Mr Chomp?' Mr Chomp lowered his massive head slowly in acknowledgement to Mr Chew's question. 'I must say though you look a little bit worse for wear, Dan, have you been through the wringer?' he asked, with a little hysterical giggle. 'It is so lovely to see you admiring the history of this lovely place. I would never have clocked the youth of today as history buffs. Game station shootings and Internet meanderings is what I would have said, not the lovely lure of people gone by. I do so love the stories of kings and queens, knights and jousting. I could see myself very easily as a noble knight striding across the countryside, bringing justice and peace. Oh, yes, I would have been a great knight. I would have had a great big broad sword that I would have sharpened on the bones of peasants. Can you imagine it, a lovely sharpening every single day? But where on earth are my manners, hello there, Clive, how lovely to meet you once again, my naughty friend.' Chew had reached the front of the church by this time and stood looking between us, waiting for an answer.

'We're searching for the coin, like we agreed back in the museum,' Abby said.

'I see, how lovely. I'm so glad you took our request seriously, Ms Abigail, that was very wise of you,' he grinned broadly his ivory teeth spreading out from bright red lips. 'And tell me, how fairs your noble endeavour?'

'We're still looking. We thought it might be here but we were wrong. There are still a few places we need to check though. This place was quite low on our list, and now we're all working together it will be much easier,' Abby said with a hint of desperation in her voice.

'Oh that's so lovely. I think it's a credit to you all that you've decided to pool your resources to solve this little conundrum. Especially you, Dan, it can't be easy for you having to help the man who shot your farther, what a trooper you are. Oh, yes, indeed you are.' Chomp continued to grin manically as he spoke, tiny strands of greasy black hair drooping across his forehead. 'I wasn't there at the time of the shooting you understand. But I hear you were, Dan, so tell me, what was it like? Was there much blood? I hear it looks extra bright in the fierce sun, is that correct? What did it smell like, Dan? Could you smell the fear dripping out of your dad along with his life's blood? I bet you could.' He shuffled further forward as he ask each question, his eyes on fire, his lips quivering with each syllable.

'You're insane, Chew,' was all I could reply through the revulsion.

'Yes, of course I am, you silly little boy, it's why I'm so good at my job,' he replied, chuckling. 'If I wasn't you would have been caught long ago. Now please show me the coin, children, and don't pretend you don't have it, I saw you holding it when I arrived. You wouldn't have phoned us and told us to meet you here if you didn't think you would find the coin.'

There was a moment of silence as the fates decided the next move in the game. Abby stepped forward and dropped the fake coin into Chew's outstretched hand.

He grabbed it quickly, winking at me as he did, then reached into his pocket and took out a small eye glass with a light blue coloured lens. He popped this into his right eye and brought up the coin and examined it closely, tenderly turning it over several times and rubbing it slowly between his thumb and forefinger. Eventually satisfied he sighed and flicked the coin back at Abby.

'Now give me the real one Abigail,' he said with a frustrated sigh.

'What do you mean?' she replied with a stutter.

'Don't play games with me young lady, where is it?' Chomp hissed fiercely.

'We don't have it,' she replied quietly, staring down at her shoes.

'It would be most unfortunate for you if you didn't.'

She took a large swallow then looked up at him, defiance spreading across her face. 'We have until tomorrow afternoon, you said that and I thought you were a man of your word.'

'I am indeed, but it would appear that you are not a girl of your word. You clearly don't have it and by the looks of you all you have no idea how to get it. I don't think it matters how long I give you, you'll never get that coin, will you, Abigail?'

'I might,' she replied curtly.

'I don't work on mights, I work on wills and will nots. We especially like will nots, they takes us into really exciting places. So what was your plan? Palm the fake off on us and hope we wouldn't notice? That was very silly of you Abigail.'

'No we wouldn't do that, we're just as surprised as you are that it's a fake,' she drew a sharp intake of breath and covered her mouth with her hand as she realized what she'd said.

'Did you hear that Mr Chomp, they didn't know it was a fake? Oh dear me, that means they thought this was the real one. They must have come to this lovely church expecting it was here. Did you find it somewhere amongst the pews? Was Dan here helping you too? I bet you were devastated to find that it isn't real, am I right?' he asked with a throaty chuckle. 'You have no idea where it is, do you, Abigail? That's what you didn't want to tell me, isn't it? You and Clive were pinning all your hopes on this being the real one and now that it isn't, you're stumped; how delicious.'

'We'll find it,' was all she could whisper

'No, I don't think you will,' he replied, drawing his vicious flick knife from his pocket. 'Clive's had so many more chances than we have ever given anyone else and it's led to nothing but disappointment. I'm not sure we will ever get over it. Perhaps finding out the colour of his intestines might help, what do you think, Mr Chomp?' He stepped forward menacingly tapping the tip of the blade against the top of one of the pews.

'You'll never get the coin if you kill me,' Clive said, stepping back from the advancing monster.

'Perhaps not, but it will be fun slicing you up, Clive. I'll enjoy watching you scream and thrash as I rummage about inside your belly. Do you know how long the large intestine is? It's long enough to use as a scarf. That'll look quite nice on you.' He continued to tap the top of the pew with the knife as he spoke, slowly and deliberately moving forward. We all moved back in unison, a secret part of me hoping Chew would be happy to stop with the murder of Clive.

'You wouldn't dare hurt him,' Abby moaned.

'But I would my dear Abigail, it won't be the first time Mr Chomp and I have had fun with someone's intestines. Although Mr Chomp prefers the eyeballs, he says they taste quite delicate when marinated in spices.'

'So you'd do that would you?' Clive said, suddenly moving forward. 'You'd torture and kill me in cold blood and give up any hope of ever getting the coin?'

'Sadly, yes, Clive. I'm afraid our employer would be most upset but it's a price worth paying,' Chew replied.

'You've done it before you say?' Clive asked stopping just in front of Mr Chew.

'Many times. Why only yesterday we helped a naughty farmer meet his maker. He was most upset about a stolen jeep and a combine, but he just wouldn't see reason. Mr Chomp opened up his throat and all was right with the world once again. You should have seen all the lovely blood, Dan. Far more than what spilled out of your dad no doubt. It turned his horrible checky shirt a lovely deep red.' Chomp looked almost wistful as he recounted the horrors he'd inflicted the day before. I drew a deep breath and tried not to panic. These two monsters had clearly killed the unfortunate farmer I'd stolen the combine from. I'd created yet one more victim of the chase.

'And you're here in the church of St Aidan just outside Bamburgh village to kill me too. Me, Clive Thornton, you're going to kill me too?' Clive continued.

'Why yes dear Clive we are, and I can tell you we're going to enjoy it,' Chew replied with a grin.

'Then you better get on with it because the police are on their way and they heard every word you said, dear Mr Chew,' Clive responded, holding up his mobile in front of the monster's face. I could clearly see that the display was active with a current call, the number 999 showing in the corner.

Chew's face became a slab of white stone, his eyes dead, and his tiny moustache frozen. 'You shouldn't have done that,' he said darkly. He launched himself at Clive, bringing his cane down across his shoulder. Clive yelled in pain and tried to step away but the monster was on him quickly. Chew let out a tiny mewl as he hit Clive's body. They both went down with him on top, the knife flashing towards Clive's face, his cane clattering away down one of the aisles. Abby screamed and fell backwards, hitting the side of a pew as she went. I stood frozen to the spot, suddenly unsure of what to do. Clive was no ally but Chew was a monster. I was caught between diving in to help him and turning to run away.

The fighters wrestled on the floor for a moment, Clive holding Chew's knife hand at bay with an effort. They both huffed and hissed at each other, Chew's face turning a fiery red with the strain. Slowly he began to get the upper hand and the knife blade began to lower towards Clive's eyeball.

'The eyeball pops when a blade pierces it, Clive, it pops right across your face,' Chew hissed, his tiny moustache quivering as he pressed down on the knife handle as hard as he could. Clive began to blow spit bubbles out of his mouth, his cheeks turning purple, a slow whining noise escaping from between his teeth as he pushed against the knife hand with all his remaining strength. It was clear that Chew had the upper hand and the blade was going to strike through Clive's eye in a matter of moments.

Without thinking I dived forward and into Chew, smashing him sideways and into the side of a pew. The heavy wooden seat screeched backwards with the impact and clattered into its neighbour. Chew rocked back onto his feet quickly and looked at me with murder in his eyes.

'You'll pay for that, Danny boy,' he growled, before lifting the wicked flick knife up in front of his face and waving it slowly at me. I scrambled backwards on my bottom, trying to get away before he could reach me with the blade, but Chew quickly launched himself towards me with a scream, diving over Clive's horizontal form, the blade held out in front of him, the steel flashing red, then blue then green as it pierced the light cascading down from one of the stain glass windows behind me. My back hit the side of another pew and I stopped with nowhere to go, a split second away from becoming a Chew kebab. Just before the flying monster reached me with his blade he stopped and plummeted downwards, Clive's hands wrapped around his ankles. He yelled in frustration and slashed the blade behind him, desperately trying to cut his attacker, but Clive managed to remain out of the blade's way as he held onto Chew's legs.

It was a desperate move with only one real outcome. If he was able to turn around properly, Chew would be able to plunge the knife into Clive. He knew this and held onto his ankles with all his strength. They wrestled for a few moments, Chew trying to kick his ankles free while slashing his blade behind him, Clive gripping the ankles with all his strength and trying to stay out of the way of the flashing blade. It would have made a comical scene if it hadn't been so deadly.

From the corner of my eye, I could see Mr Chomp unfold his arms and slowly walk towards us in a calm, almost casual, manner. I knew it would be all over much quicker if the man mountain reached Clive. Nothing would be able to stand in his way, but trying to interfere right now might get me stabbed. Before I could decide my next move, however, Abby's foot passed before my eyes and connected with Chew's blade hand. The knife clattered away into the darkness.

Chew screamed in surprise and pain, grabbing his hand close to his chest. Clive instantly let go of his ankles and scrambled to his feet, moving to stand beside Abby, his hands on his knees, head bowed as he tried to catch his breath.

'What is going on here?' a voice rumbled from the side of the church. Suddenly a red-faced vicar strode into view, his eyes bulging, his cassock flapping as he raced around the edge of the seats, trying to get to us as quickly as he could. 'This is God's house, a place of peace. What do you think you're doing?' he demanded.

Before he could get any closer Mr Chomp suddenly appeared over him, looking down with cold, dead eyes.

'Who are you?' the vicar asked.

Chomp slashed a knife across the priest's neck in reply, then turned his attention back to us. The priest clutched at his neck, gurgling noises escaping from his throat. Rich, red blood dribbled over the tops of his hands, then became a torrent turning them a deep red and changing the front of his cassock a shiny black. He staggered backwards for a few strides, eyes pleading with us, bubbles of blood escaping from his mouth, then he collapsed to the floor, his head hitting the hard stone with a thump.

Abby gasped and staggered backward, her hand covering her mouth. Clive just stood where he was and stared at the crumpled body now surrounded by an ever increasing pool of blood. I slowly got to my feet and leaned against the side of a pew, too stunned to trust that I could stand on my own.

Chew rose to his feet and brushed his suit carefully, checking that every speck of dirt has been removed.

'Oh, dear, look at what you've done, Clive?' he said after a few more moments of preening.

'What?' Clive responded dully.

'Look at what you've done. If you'd just come quietly, you wouldn't have forced Mr Chomp to send that nice priest on his way. I can't believe how naughty you are.'

Your friend killed him, you maniac,' Clive whispered.

'Yes, but he wouldn't have had to if you'd been a good boy and come quietly.'

'So you can kill me?'

'So we can give you your punishment. Now we're going to have to punish all of you for interfering and because naughty Clive has called the law. You are a silly boy.'

'No one's getting punished today,' Abby said, raising her gun and pointing it at the two monsters.

'Whoa, she's got a gun!' Chew said, clapping his hands and gurgling like a child. 'What do you think you're going to do with that dear? Are you going to shoot me or Mr Chomp? You see you won't have time to kill us both and whoever you miss will certainly make mincemeat of you and your little friends. This is fun,' he sighed.

'How do you know I won't get you both?' Abby replied shakily, her gun hand dipping up and down in front of her?

Chew barked out a quick, forceful laugh then clapped his hands again. 'You're an amateur, but you've got spirit, I'll give you that. Perhaps I'll kill you quickly just for your cheek. Clive will experience all our love, however,' he said, turning his eyes towards him and licking his red lips slowly.

By this time, Mr Chomp had arrived and stood quietly beside Mr Chew, his hands resting by his sides, small droplets of the vicar's blood dripping from a wicked looking razor blade he held delicately between his fingers.

'Your move, children,' Chew said, his eyes bright. For a moment we all stood still, none of us wanting to be the one to crack. I vainly hoped we could stand there long enough for the police to arrive, but I knew they only came at the end when everything had been decided, just like in the movies.

Suddenly, Chew jumped forward and raised his hands above his head.

'Boo!' he yelled. Abby screamed and the gun went off. Chew was thrown backwards as the bullet hit him square in the chest, sending him reeling over the back of a pew.

Mr Chomp let out a high pitched scream and scrambled after Chew. Abby screamed at the same time and dropped the gun, stepping backwards with her hands covering her mouth.

'Oh my God!' Clive yelled, striding over to check on the wounded monster.

Abby continued to step backwards, her head shaking from side to side. I remained frozen to the spot, partly unable and partly unwilling to help Abby or Clive and praying for the sound of sirens. I could see the back of Clive's coat leaning over the edge of the pew, his messy head out of sight, one arm running along the length of the wooden seat for balance. The odd sob and squeal rose up from the spot taking Clive's attention and I could vaguely hear him mouthing words of concern or comfort. Why, I don't know; the two monsters were preparing to slice us all open just moments before.

Suddenly his arm began to shake and then it disappeared. His torso surged forward then back as he wrestled with something behind the pew. His feet banged against the seat behind him, sending it lurching forward. The back of his head bobbed into view then fell back down behind the back of the pew, his left arm flailing around then crashing back down again with a slap. Suddenly he surged to his feet like a bullet shot from a gun and fell backwards into the pew behind him. It broke his fall as it screeched against the stone floor. He fell sideways onto it, laying there unmoving like some child's forgotten toy.

Mr Chomp rose from behind the pew, his face a mess of tears and snot. His eyes a puffy red, his bottom lip quivering. He held the still form of Mr Chew delicately between his massive arms, and stood there for a moment, wailing like a lost child. 'Look at what you've done,' he moaned. 'Look at the lovely flower you've crushed. How could you do that, how could you take him away from me?' He began to shake again, looking down at the still form in his arms with a mixture of longing, love and agony etched across his massive features.

'It's all gone wrong,' he whispered to Chew's body. 'It's all gone wrong and I don't know how to fix it.'

Suddenly, he looked up and stared straight at Abby, his eyes full of murder, a single tear dripping from the end of his nose. 'This is all you fault isn't it? You're the one to blame. I'm going to crush you for this.' he said quietly, taking a threatening step forward, the corpse rocking in his arms as he did.

'Stay back!' she wailed, taking a step backwards.

Mr Chomp laughed lightly, the sound reverberating off the cold stone walls. 'Look at you, girly, ordering me around.' He took another step forward, his mean eyes bright, his cruel mouth tilted upwards in a wicked grin. 'This is going to be fun, eh Mr Chew? We're going to make the little girly scream.' He let the still form of his friend slowly slip from his grasp. The body fell to the floor with a dull thud, leaving a trail of wet, dark blood running down Chomp's immaculate suit. He slowly raised his right hand and pointed a finger at Abby. 'I'm going to cut you with my lovely blade,' he said almost to himself.

Abby took another tentative step backwards, her eyes never leaving Mr Chomp's face.

'Abby, run!' Clive screamed

She turned and bolted towards the far end of the church and disappeared out of a side exit, the monster lumbering after her.

'I'll take care of you two later,' he promised as he rushed past.

'Abby!' Clive yelled after her, wincing as he attempted to stand and reach out to stop Chomp.

'You have to go after them, Dan, he'll kill her,' he said, turning to me with desperate eyes.

I turned to look at my former prey standing holding his arm, blood slowly creeping over his fingers, a calm washing over me despite the frenzied events of moments before.

'I can't go, I'm hurt. Please, Dan, please help her.'

I shook my head and laughed quietly. 'You want me to

help her, after everything she's done, you must be mad.'

'He's going to kill her!' Clive shouted. 'I know what she's done, Dan, but she's not evil, not like them, she was only trying to help me. Please, if you felt anything for her, help her now.'

'That's low even for you.'

'You can't let him kill her, Dan, you don't want that on your conscience, I know you don't.'

He was right. I hated the idea of Abby getting hurt, even after everything she'd done. But a part of me felt like this was just what she deserved after all the pain she'd caused.

'Please, Dan,' he said through gritted teeth, his eyes wide and pleading.

'That's a maniac going after her, why do you think I'd get in his way?'

'You have to help her, Danny; it's the right thing to do,' my dad responded. This was a hell of a time for my dad to return, but he was right, or at least that part of my brain was.

'Please!' was all Clive could say.

I shook my head and sighed, 'Okay, but she goes to the cops straight afterwards.'

Clive nodded his head and plopped back down on the pew.

'Don't even think about moving, Clive; you need to go to the hospital and then to prison. I'll come after you if you do.'

'I'm staying here, just try and save my sister,' he replied, his voice urgent.

I turned away from him and started to jog towards the back of the church.

'Okay, one more chase,' I said to the wind, to my dad and to myself, heading towards to exit.

23 - I CAPTURE THE CASTLE

I stepped out into the light and ran across the graveyard, hoping to see Abby bobbing away in the distance but seeing only rows of neat gravestones stretching away and a series of sand dunes hugging the perimeter wall. A wrought iron gate swung open on the breeze, intermittently squeaking a loud refrain. It was the only exit this side of the church and clearly the way Abby and Chomp had gone.

Racing through it, I began wading up and over soft sand, the castle appearing and disappearing in the middle distance as I went. I was hoping that Chomp hadn't caught up with her but I had no idea what I was going to do if I caught up with them. I was no fighter and Chomp was a man mountain who thrilled at the pain of others. I squeezed my hands tightly as I imagined the priest holding his neck, blood pumping between his figures and slowly spreading across his cassock.

To my surprise, I felt the cold hard ridges of the gun and looked down to see it sitting snugly in my tightening hand. I had no memory of picking it up as I left the church but I knew this must be the gun Abby discarded right after she shot Chew. I looked at its dark black cylinder and wondered how many times it had been aimed at someone with the intention to kill.

'Abby shot me with that gun, Dan,' my dad exclaimed. I scrambled to a stop, the image of the dying priest quickly forgotten and stared down at the sleek black pistol. Revulsion and curiosity raging through me in equal measure. This had been how it started. This bleak piece of metal had taken my dad away from me and set me on the path to madness. 'The gun didn't kill me, Dan, it was the desperate girl that did that and you have to go and help her now.'

I knew he was right, this was just a cold bit of steel, an inanimate object without feeling or thought, but it still burned in my hand and I was convinced it would turn me into a killer too if I held it too long. I raised my arm back and prepared to launch the thing into the air when a splash of red, the colour of Abby's blouse, appeared above a sand dune, bobbed along behind strands of tall grass for a brief moment, then it disappeared.

Suddenly, I was racing after them without a second thought. My dad was right, I had to go and save her. This was my world and I welcomed it with open arms. Even though I'd only lived it since yesterday it was as natural as breathing now. My body became calm, my mind focused, my breathing regular and long, my strides wide and as even as possible along the soft sand.

The gun still sat heavy in my hand but I was loathe to discard it now; after all I would probably need it to kill a monster.

'You're right, Danny, you'd better shoot him as quick as you can, you can do it, my bright boy,' the wind said as it caressed my cheek and gently pushed me along the ridge of the latest dune. I tumbled down its face and saw Abby reach the top of the one in front, Chomp only a stride behind her.

I got up and raced towards the rising dune as fast as I could, desperate to reach them before Chomp could use his wicked blade. I increased my strides and panted up to the top of the hill, dived over without a pause and tumbled down the sleek, soft sand, losing my footing halfway and falling down the rest of the dune. As I reached the bottom, sand flying all around me, I hit something hard, sending it sprawling to the ground with a scream.

Chomp rolled over twice and scrambled to a stop, his fingers clawing into the soft earth. I came to an awkward stop a few metres away, my shoulders and neck complaining about the fall.

A guttural roar tumbled out of his mouth as he got to his knees and crouched with hands held out on either side of him. He remained there for a brief moment, panting hard and then launched himself at me. I barely had time to get to my knees before he hit me square in the chest with his shoulder. I was sent reeling backwards into the sloping dune. He scrambled on top of me and slapped me hard across the face before drawing the cutthroat down my cheek.

I roared in pain and lifted the gun in a wide arc, the handle smashing into the side of his skull, sending him tumbling off me. I lifted my fingers to my cheek and brushed the wound lightly; they came away slick with blood. I turned to see Abby lying at the bottom of the dune, her eyes bright with fear, her mouth a thin line. I took a step towards her but stopped as Chomp staggered to his feet uncertainly, blood running freely from a large gash on the side of his head.

'I'm going to kill you,' he said groggily.

I raised the gun and pointed it at his chest. 'I don't think you are.'

'You think that little thing will stop me?' he asked with a chuckle.

I licked my lips and looked down through the barrel of the pistol. My arm shook from the top of my shoulder to the tips of my icy fingers, each one latched tightly around the grip of the sleek black, weapon. The wind caressed them gently, shivering over the scratches and cuts, tickling my blackened nails, caressing my thumb, and urging my trigger finger to press down slowly. Intermittent gusts pushed at the small of my back, rocking me forward, then back, shaking my stance and rocking my gun arm.

'Why are you doing this? You're not going to get what you want now, you must know that? People have died, the police are on their way and you've got nothing to show for all the pain and suffering you've caused. You might as well turn and run, it's your only chance.'

'The pain and suffering is what I want don't you understand?'

'Yeah, I know that. I know you're nothing but a monster, but this all stops now. I've got the gun, remember.'

'You're not going to kill me. You don't have it in you. I've seen how you operate. You wouldn't hurt a fly. You don't have the strength. It takes a special kind of courage to shoot someone and all I see stood in front of me is a coward. A coward who would chase someone across the countryside rather than face up to what they have to do. I'm worth ten of you and you know it. I wouldn't have even asked; you'd be dead right now if I was standing in your place.'

I pulled the hammer back and prepared to squeeze the trigger. The wind gusted again and whispered through the tall grass surrounding us. It whipped around my trouser legs and wrapped my shirt tightly around me. It urged me forward, it urged me to pull the trigger and it demanded that the chase come to an end.

'You think it takes courage to shoot someone?' I gasped. 'It doesn't take courage; it takes rage!'

I squeezed the trigger hard and a moment of fire exploded from the cylinder. The gun recoiled in my hand, jumping upwards and sending my gun arm reaching for the sky. The blast ricocheted outwards, echoing around the sand dunes and fanning through the grass. The sand exploded next to Chomp's foot and he was forced to jump backwards, a scream splitting his lips. He quickly regained his composure and turned towards me, rage flashing across his face, turning his cheeks a deep purple and making the veins stand out on his forehead.

He let out a guttural roar and dived forward, launching the blood smeared blade as he did. The gun exploded for a second time, punching a ragged black hole in the centre of Chomp's chest. The force of the impact pushing him backwards and onto the ground. He lay there for a moment, weakly trying to lift himself upwards and then he let out a sigh and went still.

I felt numb as I watched him die, my brain not able to comprehend what had happened.

'You killed a monster, Dan, it was him or you,' my dad whispered.

'I guess you took care of him,' Abby said weakly from the floor, coughing at the effort.

'No!' I yell, diving towards her.

She lay there, her face a mask of shock and pain, her eyes staring at a spot high in the sky, her hands holding her chest, trying desperately to stop the blood that was flowing through her fingers. I took hold of her gently and cradle her in my arms.

'Oh my God no,' I sobbed.

'You did it, Dan,' she said weakly.

'We told you to end the chase, Danny and you did, what a clever boy,' said the wind. 'Now you've got it all, now you've captured the castle. What an amazing boy you are and a murderer too, welcome to the club,' the breeze cackled, running along my spine and tickling the nap of my neck.

'If it's over, you should go.' I reply through a mess of Abby's hair, lifting my head and expecting to see an impudent demon flying about above me but only seeing the unrelenting blue sky. I looked down to see Abby staring at me calmly, her delicate grey eyes soft and inviting for once.

'Who are you talking to, Dan?' she whispered.

'Just myself, there's no one else here.'

'You've been doing that a lot lately did you know?'

'Yeah, I know, it's helped. Don't move, Abby, I'll go and get help, just don't move.'

'No, please don't leave me, I don't want to be on my own,' she replied urgently.

'I'm sorry but I have to go and get help, you're hurt,' I sobbed, tears trickling down my dirty face.

'It's really cold, Dan, please hold me, I'm so cold,' she pleaded weakly. I gently pulled her close and felt a warm stain spread across my chest.

'It's over, isn't it?' she whispered

'No, you're going to be fine,' I replied.

'I love it here, did I ever tell you that? I love the castle and the sea, they're magic. I always liked it best when I was with you. It seems empty when you're not here, like there's a part of me missing,' she said quietly.

'Don't talk, save your strength. They'll be here soon and everything will be okay, I promise,' I reply unconvincingly.

'I remember the fun we had racing around the King's Hall, don't you? What was the name of that horrible woman in blue who kept chasing us out?'

'Mrs Wilkins,' I whispered.

'Yeah, that was it,' she chuckled, coughing deeply afterwards. 'She was a real cow, but it was fun though, it was always fun,' she said with a sigh.

'You were always fun,' I replied. 'Especially when you were getting your own way, which was pretty much all of the time, wasn't it?'

I wait for her to answer but there was only silence.

I lowered her gently and arranged her hair as neatly as my trembling hands would let me; she always liked to be neat and tidy.

I stared down at her serene face and sighed as a single tear dropped from my lashes and fell onto her pale white cheek. With another sigh I turned around and began to walk out of the sand dunes. 'I won't be long, Abby, just got one more chase to finish,' I said, hobbling towards the flashes of blue splashing across the castle walls and the sounds of sirens stretching across the sky.

Epilogue - The Sounds of Sirens

The cricket pitch stretched away from me, surrounded on three sides by a wall of houses, every one turned electric blue by the beacons winking insistently in front of them. The castle loomed on my left, a brooding giant casting its own gloom. At the far side of the pitch, I could see cops in Hi-Vis vests talking urgently amongst themselves. I knew it wouldn't be long before they saw me, then the chase would finally come to an end but I hoped to take a last moment of freedom before then, to say goodbye.

I looked up at the towering presence above me as I hobbled over the neatly trimmed lawn. It seemed like the castle had linked us all in the chase from the very beginning. It had always held its treasures safe, my dad had seen to that and now it looked like it would keep our memories safe too. Somehow, I wasn't sure how, my dad had managed to put the coin back where it belonged. For some reason, only known to himself, he'd decided to put a fake coin inside the box containing St Oswald's right arm. Probably to put Clive off the scent if he got too insistent on getting the coin. I didn't need to go back into the castle to check that the real coin was there. It would be, it was the right thing to do to. Dad always protected his friend and family, it was typical of him.

'You did everything you could, Dan, she just couldn't

be saved.'

'Yeah, I know, look after her, Dad, she's going to need your help,' I reply, glad for once that he returned to my mind. Glad that I was just mad enough to hear him. His voice was faint, dying away now the chase was nearly finished. I didn't need him anymore; a good lawyer on the other hand looked like it was going to be essential.

'Do you think they'll let me go to your funeral, Dad?'

'It will be all alright as long as you tell the truth that was their flaw from the very beginning; they just needed to tell the truth.'

'I've got one hell of a lot of truths to tell them. I just hope they listen,' I reply, hobbling over the pitch in the middle of the field.

'I'm so sorry I couldn't save you, I let you down.'

'No, I let you down, Dan. I should have told you everything from the beginning, that was my flaw,' he replied, the soft echo of his voice rattling around my mind.

'I wish you were real, Dad. I wish you were still moaning about the youth of today, goodbye, I love you.'

I hobbled to a stop two thirds of the way across the pitch and stopped to catch my breath. I could still smell her perfume caressing my cheeks and wondered for a moment if she'd be there, if I turned around. Glaring at me with her arms crossed and that disappointed look on her face. I knew it was a foolish idea but hope is the last thing to die, my dad always said.

I turned around slowly and thought I saw a flash of red disappearing around the edge of the castle wall.

'Have fun, Abby, and look out for Mrs Wilkins, she can be a real devil if she catches you chasing around the outer ward.'

I turned back towards the flashing blue and started on the last leg of the chase. I knew it was going to be easy this time, after all no one was trying to shoot me.

Other titles by BLKDOG Publishing for your consideration:

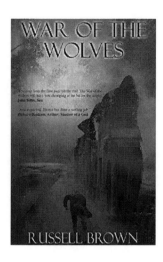

War of the Wolves
By Russell Brown

Lewis saw the wolf because he couldn't sleep.

Lewis didn't believe in magic. Not until he was chased by a man who could change into a wolf. Not until he discovered he could change into one too. Not until he was told that he and his friend Charlie were the only ones that stood between a demon and the end of the world as they knew it. Now he believes. Now he has no choice.

Now he'll need to learn what it means to be a magical creature in a secret world at war. Now he'll need to discover how to control his new found magical powers, and learn how to fight monsters, hell bent on trying to destroy everything he loves. The only problem is, it's sometimes hard to know who the monsters really are.

War of the Wolves, book one of *The Demon Gatekeeper* trilogy, is a nerve-jangling ride, through the heart of a secret magical world, existing right underneath our noses.

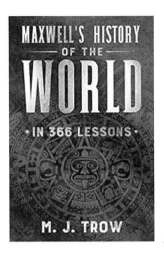

Maxwell's History of the World in 366 Lessons
By M. J. Trow

Peter Maxwell is the History teacher you wish you'd had. If you meet anyone (and you will) who says 'I hate History. It's boring,' they weren't taught by Mad Max.

Many of you will know him as the crime-solving sleuth (along with his police-person wife, Jacquie) in the Maxwell series by M.J. Trow (along with *his* non-policeperson wife, Carol, aka Maryanne Coleman – uncredited!) but what he is *paid* to do is teach History. And to that end has brought – and continues to bring – culture to thousands.

In his 'blog' (Dinosaur Maxwell doesn't really know what that is) written in 2012, the year in which the world was supposed to end, but mysteriously didn't, you will find all sorts of fascinating factoids about the *only* important subject on the school curriculum. So, if you weren't lucky enough to be taught by Max, or you've forgotten all the History you ever knew, here is your chance to play catch-up. The 'blog' has been edited by Maxwell's friend, the crime writer M.J. Trow, who writes almost as though he knows what the Great Man was thinking.

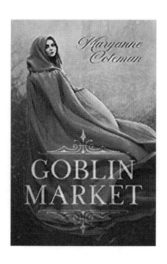

Goblin Market
By Maryanne Coleman

Have you ever wondered what happened to the faeries you used to believe in? They lived at the bottom of the garden and left rings in the grass and sparkling glamour in the air to remind you where they were. But that was then − now you might find them in places you might not think to look. They might be stacking shelves, delivering milk or weighing babies at the clinic. Open your eyes and keep your wits about you and you might see them.

But no one is looking any more and that is hard for a Faerie Queen to bear and Titania has had enough. When Titania stamps her foot, everyone in Faerieland jumps; publicity is what they need. Television, magazines. But that sort of thing is much more the remit of the bad boys of the Unseelie Court, the ones who weave a new kind of magic; the World Wide Web. Here is Puck re-learning how to fly; Leanne the agent who really is a vampire; Oberon's Boys playing cards behind the wainscoting; Black Annis, the bag-lady from Hainault, all gathered in a Restoration comedy that is strictly twenty-first century.

Prester John: Africa's Lost King
By Richard Denham

He sits on his jewelled throne on the Horn of Africa in the maps of the sixteenth century. He can see his whole empire reflected in a mirror outside his palace. He carries three crosses into battle and each cross is guarded by one hundred thousand men. He was with St Thomas in the third century when he set up a Christian church in India. He came like a thunderbolt out of the far East eight centuries later, to rescue the crusaders clinging on to Jerusalem. And he was still there when Portuguese explorers went looking for him in the fifteenth century.

He went by different names. The priest who was also a king was Ong Khan; he was Genghis Khan; he was Lebna Dengel. Above all, he was a Christian king who ruled a vast empire full of magical wonders: men with faces in their chests; men with huge, backward-facing feet; rivers and seas made of sand. His lands lay next to the earthly Paradise which had once been the Garden of Eden. He wrote letters to popes and princes. He promised salvation and hope to generations.

But it was noticeable that as men looked outward, exploring more of the natural world; as science replaced superstition and the age of miracles faded, Prester John was always elsewhere. He was beyond the Mountains of the Moon, at the edge of the earth, near the mouth of Hell.

Was he real? Did he ever exist? This book will take you on a journey of a lifetime, to worlds that might have been, but never were. It will take you, if you are brave enough, into the world of Prester John.

Fade
By Bethan White

There is nothing extraordinary about Chris Rowan. Each day he wakes to the same faces, has the same breakfast, the same commute, the same sort of homes he tries to rent out to unsuspecting tenants.

There is nothing extraordinary about Chris Rowan. That is apart from the black dog that haunts his nightmares and an unexpected encounter with a long forgotten demon from his past. A nudge that will send Chris on his own downward spiral, from which there may be no escape.

There is nothing extraordinary about Chris Rowan...

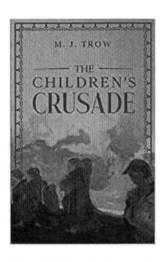

The Children's Crusade
By M. J. Trow

In the summer of 1212, 30,000 children from towns and villages all over France and Germany left their homes and families and began a crusade. Their aim; to retake Jerusalem, the holiest city in the world, for God and for Christ. They carried crosses and they believed, because the Bible told them so, that they could cross the sea like Moses. The walls of Jerusalem would fall, like Jericho's did for Joshua.

It was the age of miracles – anything was possible. Kings ignored the Children; so did popes and bishops. The handful of Church chroniclers who wrote about them were usually disparaging. They were delusional, they were inspired not by God, but the Devil. Their crusade was doomed from the start.

None of them reached Outremer, the Holy Land. They turned back, exhausted. Some fell ill on the way; others died. Others still were probably sold into slavery to the Saracens – the very Muslims who had taken Jerusalem in the first place.

We only know of three of them by name – Stephen, Nicholas and Otto. One of them was a shepherd, another a ploughboy, the third a scholar. The oldest was probably fourteen. Today, in a world where nobody believes in miracles, the Children of 1212 have almost been forgotten.

Almost… but not quite…

The poet Robert Browning caught the mood in his haunting poem, *The Pied Piper of Hamelin*, bringing to later readers the sad image of a lost generation, wandering a road to who knew where.

www.blkdogpublishing.com

Printed in Great Britain
by Amazon

55669566R00118